THE TREE HOUSE
and Other Stories

THE TREE HOUSE
and Other Stories

Collin Johnson

Dolphin in the West, Inc.
New York

Additional copies of *The Tree House*
are available direct from the publisher
Dolphin in the West, Inc.
527 Third Ave., Suite 302
New York, NY 10016

Published by Dolphin in the West, Inc.
527 Third Avenue, Suite 302
New York, NY 10016

Made and printed in the United States of America

Designed, set in type, and produced by John Beck,
        editor and book producer, Wilkes-Barre, Pa.
Manufactured by Quinn-Woodbine Inc., Woodbine, N. J.
Cover printed by Zodiac, Wilkes-Barre, Pa.

10   9   8   7   6   5   4   3   2   1

To Sarah

Contents

Preface

This collection of plays and short stories was first broadcast on BBC Radio 4. I grew up listening to the radio,
and when I was involved in a writing project it was always
part of my working day.

The BBC would broadcast a play a day Monday to Friday in the afternoons; then there was Saturday playhouse,
the Monday play, and at various points over the years there
have also been other play slots. When it comes to short stories, there has been a long custom of a new short story every weekday. Where else have writers been so encouraged?
Upward of three hundred new plays and prose pieces a
year are commissioned and produced. Sadly now, these fine
traditions are being eroded. Constraints of time, money, and
space now all threaten this superb structure.

Travels with Henry was my first broadcast, and tells the
story of my first job as a professional actor. After that, I
began to write fiction. Not unusually, several of the pieces
contain elements developed from my own experience. *Cold
Call* was the result of two desperate weeks trying to sell
advertising. *Capital Gains* grew out of an accusatory letter

from my own bank. "Dear Mr. Johnson," wrote the bank, "It has come to our notice that your ten-pound cashcard faciliity is overdrawn. Please remedy this situation at your earliest opportunity."

I enjoyed this letter. I was sharing a flat with a law student at the time; and together we concocted a reply:

"Dear Sir," (we wrote)

"Thank you for your letter of the first instance. On seeing the opening sentence, it fell from my nerveless fingers. Was I again reading someone else's mail? A swift glance at the address reassured me on this point but gave rise to certain doubts as to your competence. I do not have, nor have I ever had, a ten-pound cashcard facility. I am, as you may know, a starving student, and the idea that someone is throwing my money around with this gay abandon fills me with a nameless dread. Should this tendency continue, doubtless you will find me, third bench along, underneath the arches, Charing Cross Station."

We were pleased with this letter, and when the bank sent a craven apology for the mistake, we felt pretty smug about the whole business. So it was a bad move on my part to get genuinely overdrawn shortly afterwards. The bank ruthlessly pressed its advantage, sending increasingly ferocious letters daily for about six weeks. Eventually, I got a job and paid off the debt. But things would never be the same with me and the bank—too much bitterness had passed between us. They showed no sorrow when I took my business elsewhere.

I wrote *The Tree House* when I was already a father and had learned that one of the lines I use in the play is true: "When you have children, you love more than you knew you had love in you." Finally, *Further Travels with Henry* is, like its predecessor, a memoir.

Acknowledgments

M y heartfelt thanks to Andy Jordan, my producer at BBC Radio 4, who has tirelessly championed the cause of new writing there, as well as with his own company Bristol Express.

Thanks are also due to my fellow actors who gave such excellent work in the productions of the three plays published in this volume. In order of appearance, they are: in *The Tree House* (originally broadcast as *The Inheritance*), Tom Lawrence, David Neal, George Parsons, Jilly Bond, Tim Pigott-Smith, and Jo Anderson; in *Capital Gains*, Celestine Randall, Peter Whitman, and Peter Jones; in *Cold Call*, Alistair MacGowan, David Verrey, Alice Arnold, Deborah Findlay, Shirley Dixon, Kim Wall, and Sean Baker.

THE TREE HOUSE
and Other Stories

Travels with Henry

Travels with Henry

IF YOU'RE AN ACTOR you many not be able to remember your last job, but you always remember your first one. While I was at drama school in London, I put together a one-man version of Shakespeare's play *Henry V*. I knew there was a theatre on the Isle of Mull in the Hebrides, I knew it was just outside the village of Dervaig at the western end of the island, eleven miles from the nearest bus stop. I thought this might be the place to start off.

I wrote to the people who had lived and worked there for twenty years, asking them if there was any chance that I could play my one-man *Henry V* at their theatre. Barrie and Marianne Hesketh were making a rare visit to London to collect their M.B.E.s (Member of the British Empire). We met at the Central School of Speech and Drama, where I was training and where they had trained in the days of the school's residency at the Royal Albert Hall. They were both then about fifty years old. Barrie had the air of Prospero on a bad day, thick silver hair swept backwards from a craggy forehead. Marianne looked like Judy Garland might have looked if she had gone on to bake a lot of chocolate cakes.

They began talking at once. Their conversation was not easy to follow, because they spoke as twins speak, dovetailing thoughts and sentences. I felt the conversation was going well, and I listened attentively, keen for employment. I slipped my hand into my pocket.

"You don't smoke do you?" asked Marianne. "We always ask," she said.

"No," I said. And I left the cigarette unseen in its packet. They asked if they could see me do something, and because there was never any space at the Central School of Speech and Drama, I took them to the car park, where I lustily summoned a muse of fire. It began to rain. The audition was a success—they offered me a job. It meant giving up smoking, but it was a job and brought the treasured Equity card. I bought an old leather trunk for my props and an old green car to carry them in. I gave the car a name, because I knew that a car will run for you if you love it. I called the car Henry and the clutch went. I got the clutch fixed and called the car Molly, and we've been friends ever since.

It was May when I arrived in Oban in the Western Highlands and took the ferry across the Firth of Lorn to Mull. At that time of year the rhododendrons are in full bloom. I drove the long way round the island, my vision assaulted by the vivid pinks and purples, until I came to the theatre valley. Looking over the valley, there was no sign of a theatre or any habitation. The theatre stood in a Scots acre, and a hundred years ago the minister who had lived there had planted his land with broadleaf trees—alders, limes, and beeches, and at the front and back gates to the property a rowan tree. Amongst the trees stood the house where the Heskeths had raised their family, and on the other side of the acre was the byre where the minister had kept his animals. This had now become the smallest professional theatre in Great Britain.

In one half of the byre, a horse had lived. That became the auditorium. The other half, once a cow's dwelling, had become the stage, with seating for thirty-seven people—at the back a long bench with cushions; at the front six low-slung easy chairs with springs long gone; in between, stalls from an old cinema. The six rows of audience slanted from stage level at the front to roof level at the back. The stage was ten feet wide by fifteen deep, covered with corn-colored rush matting well worn, and complete with wings, flies, blacks, tabs, one entrance stage right, and one more up-stage center. It was a theatre in miniature.

The day I arrived, Barrie and Marianne were at dress rehearsal for their new play, *Ostrich*, a two-handed piece they had written themselves. Together they had attempted everything from William Shakespeare to Michael Frayn. Some years they employed other actors, and the company had once been as huge as five. Usually they found ways to fill their stage with characters alone—this season included a two-actor version of *The Importance of Being Ernest*. After so long constantly working together they had a rapport that was fascinating to watch.

During a tea break, Marianne jokingly explained that she'd had a mastectomy. "It's the left, no the right one," she said, patting each side as if not really sure. I almost believed that she could have forgotten, but a few weeks later, as we were drinking gin after the show, I asked her about the illness. She said she could cope with it, and as regards dying she "made her arrangements." Then suddenly, "I hate the mutilation." When she said "hate," her lips trembled and tears came to her eyes.

The season opened with a performance of *Ostrich*. It was a comedy set in academia. The theatre was full. A first-night atmosphere, a party. There were friends, holiday makers, the milkman, and Betty. Betty was an indomitable lady of robust old age who lived with two boisterous dalmatians and lots of ducks in a well-kept cottage where she painted flowers. In her blue mini, she sat ramrod straight and drove at speed around the island. When she arrived at the theatre, she called "Hello dear" to whomever she met. She was the theatre's honorary grandmother, and she always brought duck eggs.

The performance was a success. There was only one interruption when a flock of sheep passed by the west wall of the theatre and I was sent to chase them away, and this became part of my job during the season. When the audience had gone, Barrie and Marianne said, "We're open!" There was a terrific sense of achievement, and off they went for the post-show drink of gin and orange juice.

A few nights later I had my own first night with *Henry V*. It was my first professional performance and I was nervous to the point of nausea, but Marianne said, "The theatre's on your side Collin, it's just told me." I believed her. The show lasted ninety minutes and there were fourteen people in the audience. The idea was to start with a bare stage and end up with it covered in the debris of the story. There were puppets—three-quarters life size for the bishops, finger puppets for the heralds—a cigar puffed vigorously for the cannon and the smoke of war, a bicycle, lots of hats, a parasol, flags, streamers, confetti, and a custard pie. I made a lot of mess. When it was over, Marianne came round and embraced me, and they took me to the kitchen for supper.

"An egg?" asked Marianne.

"Two," said Barrie. "He needs two eggs." And we drank gin.

A one-man version of *Henry V* is not an easy show to sell in the inner Hebrides. To begin with, the audience figures were not encouraging. Fourteen, eleven, seven, five, three. The night I played to three people, two of them were French. I tried everything I could think of to sell the show. I put posters up around the island with adjectives like "Dazzlingly Bold!" and "Boldly Dazzling!" Once I went to the main town, Tobermory, and stood in the street wearing a silly hat and juggling tennis balls. A policeman came and watched me. After a time he said, "And tell me, do you just stand there and play with your balls?"

At last I hit upon something to improve sales. For some reason I had a suit in plum-coloured velvet. It didn't fit very well. No matter, I bounced onto the stage one night wearing this costume, juggling tennis balls, and doing my U trailer.

"Ladies and Gentlemen, your attention please! This is a U trailer, for yes! you've guessed it! a U certified version of *Henry V*. Shakespeare on a budget and as you've never seen him before. I play all the parts—several thousand—don't forget the two armies! It's here, it's now, it's fast, it's alive, it's happening in the smallest theatre in the world. Book now to avoid disappointment!"

People liked this, and within two days the bookings for *Henry* were much improved.

After a few weeks a routine of life emerged. In the mornings the three of us would meet for coffee. Barrie and Marianne concocted a brew of such strength it made your teeth shake, and they drank a lot of it. After coffee, it was administration. Neither of the Heskeths were administrators by nature or training; they did things twice, three, or four times when once would have done. Under pressure Barrie had the habit of producing a sound like a snorting whale. He was a widely gifted man. A painter, a musician, a writer, and an actor. For twenty years he had put bread on the table by working on the stage. After lunch he would paint water colours which he sold in the theatre, and the more outrageous he was about them—"I think I'll do this one in mauve"—the faster they sold. Marianne made chocolate cakes and had ideas. She thought and spoke at a great rate and had a well-stocked and scatty mind. "You could come back next year and we'll do *Hamlet* or *Sleuth*. Are you going to tour for us? Have you read Gordon Craig?" Then there were the little theatre histories. The two-handed *Tempest*, how Olivier had nearly made it to a show, how Schofield used to come. In the evenings, we would go into the theatre an hour or so before the show, lay out a display of cookbooks, bookmarks, and chocolate cakes, and spray the dressing room, foyer, and front and back stage with insect repellant in the endless battle against the Mull midges which have boots on. This was important, but occasionally you'd find a midge on stage with you and there was nothing to do except let it graze happily.

Before long it was June and the rhododendrons lost their blooms, the yellow gorse appeared bright as acrylic paint. I got to know the island. Neither Barrie or Marianne could drive, so I used to run the errands to the shops, to the bank. When free to explore, I wandered in my old green car. There was the ancient oak forest at Torloisk, the sandy beach at Calgary which is washed by the warm gulf stream. I met Nellie who lived like a guardian at the site of the petrified tree. I met an artist from south London who lived in a remote cove. When I asked him what had brought him to Mull, he said, "Magic. Nothing more, nothing less."

Iona, where I toured in July, was different again. A quarter mile of water separates it from Mull. The cloud in the region goes to Mull and the mountain. Iona is sunlit. I had to get a special permit to take the landrover across to carry my props. One of the ferrymen came and looked at me. He was a big Glaswegian, as broad as tall, ice-blue eyes and a long knife scar in his throat.

"And what are you going to do on Iona?"

"I'm going to give a performance at the Abbey."

"Is it just yourself like?"

"Yes."

He looked at the sea and thought a moment. "Now let me get this straight, it's just you, no one else, just yourself?"

"Yes."

Thought. Silence. Then, "That doesn't sound fuckin' right to me."

I performed Henry on the altar steps of the old Abbey lit by three spotlights. There was a gale outside, and twice the west doors burst open and the wind came howling down the nave.

Back to the Little Theatre. Now the season was in full swing. A profusion of wildflowers coloured the hill behind the theatre, and the place was full every night of the week. Sometimes as many as forty-eight people—well over a hundred-percent capacity. The audience came from everywhere. Once, nine people came in an open boat from the Isle of Muck—two hours at sea. I played *Henry V* to a party of schoolboys from the famous Public School at Stowe. There was a mountain man from the American Midwest, there were the local landed gentry. I don't know what Marianne put in the chocolate cakes, but everyone seemed happy. When there was a power cut one night during a performance of Chekhov's one-act comedy *The Bear*, people in the audience willingly follow-spotted us with torches. "You wouldn't get this at the RSC," said Marianne.

At the end of the month, when the gorse yielded to the foxgloves pointing upward like spears of fire, I decided to climb the mountain Ben Moore. Ben Moore is supposed to be the home of the wizard of winter who shows his presence by laying a finger of cloud on the peak. I came within fifty feet of the summit. I stood looking along the line of watershed fearing to lose myself in the mists that came and went so suddenly. From there, over the wide landscape, the moss on the rocks the colour of salmon flesh, it seemed there was a tougher feel to life than in the soft south of Britain. At last, offering my respects to the wizard, I climbed down knowing that I would return to Mull. The island is littered with standing stones, remnants of an ancient time when earth magic ran vigorously through the land. Now and then you'd happen upon some secret place in the hills or the forests where the little folk live. And there were the faces in the trees. Many of the trees on the theatre acre had faces in them. The features were easier to see at dusk, and in the fading light the trees became totem poles. There was prescience in the ether.

A few years previously the Little Theatre had produced *Macbeth* using puppets. Although the production had been very successful, the Heskeths had no fondness for it because it had been then that Marianne had been attacked by a second cancer. They subscribed to the superstition that surrounds this play. When I arrived there was no active cancer in Marianne's body, but somehow we all knew it would come again. In August I took her to be X-rayed at the island's hospital. A tumour was discovered in her spine.

Afterward, as we drove along the valley which was exploding with purple heather, she asked, "Did you know?"

"Yes," I said. "Did you?"

"Yes," she said. We drove home in silence.

Marianne went to Glasgow for radiotherapy. Barrie and I were alone at the theatre for two weeks. We did programmes of verse and stories and one-act Chekhov plays, and on the weekends, while Barrie went to visit Marianne, I did *Henry V* and Betty came with duck eggs. After Glasgow, Marianne went straight back on stage. Radiotherapy can be a shattering treatment; sometimes she was quite literally pale green waiting in the wings of the tiny theatre that had been her home for twenty years. She'd go on stage and the pallor would fall away. It was an example of courage in the theatre that I will always remember. Her method with the disease was to outface it with stubborn disregard, and to the last her mind was full of plans for the future. "I've written to the National," she said. "I've told them I'll do anything. In my condition I could play an Amazon, or I could have the other one off and they could strap a sword to me and I'd carry a spear."

Barrie would make loud defiance. "She's not dead yet," he shouted more than once.

The season ended as it had begun with a performance of *Ostrich*. The colours in the hills were different, the blood red of the rowan berries now dominant. It was Marianne's last performance there. The theatre was full, a party atmosphere. Afterward, Barrie called me on stage; I entered with a bouquet of flowers and a bottle of champagne. I made the following speech as I poured the three of us a glass: "Ladies and Gentlemen, it has been a special summer for me and the realisation of a long-held ambition to work at this theatre. I give you the Little Theatre!" And the audience chorused, "The Little Theatre!" And there was applause. When they had all gone, we lingered in the foyer making extravagant compliments to each other in the way that actors do: "Darling, you were marvellous!" Then we went over to the kitchen for a final supper of eggs, salad, and gin.

Marianne's health had been deteriorating daily; her spine had weakened to the extent that she found sitting down and getting up difficult. Everything was reworked so that on stage she was always standing, and in this condition she and Barrie went on to complete a six-week tour in Europe. Previously, on a dozen British and half a dozen European tours, they had employed someone to drive them. But this time they went by bus and train as they progressed through the one night stands. Marianne could walk, but she couldn't carry anything, so Barrie carried all the luggage, and all the props and scenery as well.

Anyone who met the Heskeths will remember them and their theatre, but I remember them for their kindness and their courage and for my first job. A final image stays with me. A few days before I left I found a sea bird with a broken wing. I put it in a box and fed it weetabix. In time the wing healed, but the bird had lost its confidence in flight. Months later, Barrie wrote and told me how he had taken it to a cliff above the sea and thrown it high into the air. For a moment it had dropped like a stone, but then flapped its wings, happy to be free once more.

The Tree House
A Sixty-Minute Radio Play

The Tree House
A Sixty-Minute Radio Play

Characters

Thomas, age 42
Arthur, some years older, his brother
Peter, age 42, Thomas's son
Felicity, late 30s, Peter's wife
Tom, age 13, Peter's son
Dr Wilson
A Nursing Sister

Thomas knows he has a few weeks to live. Helped by his brother Arthur, he makes a series of recordings for his son Peter. The recordings are to be passed on at specific times in Peter's life. The action takes place in 1962 and 1994.

SCENE 1

Tom's Diary

    Tom: 24th February 1994. It's Dad's birthday tomorrow. I don't know what to get him. He usually gets sad on his birthdays. Mum says it's because he's getting older. I don't see what's wrong with that, I want to be older. When I tell Dad that, he says, "Don't worry you will be," or "Don't wish your life away, Boy."

At least he doesn't tell me these are the best years of my life. I think I'd be happy if I was Dad's age. I wonder if I ever will be. Lots of people don't live that long. It would be stupid to be alive and not be able to do all the things you're allowed to do when you're older. Like go to bed with someone. Why do they call it "sleep with"? I mean, it's not sleeping. Or drinking. Dad never lets me drink. Maybe I'll ask him for one tomorrow. I know what he'll say, that's the sort of question he can answer.

Last week I asked him what happens when we die. He said that different people believe different things, and I said, "But what do you think?"

Then he did one of his quiet thinking things, and he said, "I don't know Tom." What use is that?

Scene 2 (1962)

A Solicitor's Office. Arthur is reading his brother Thomas's will.

Arthur: This is the last will and testament of Thomas Douglas Davies. Being of sound mind and body, I hereby revoke all former wills and codicils made by me, and appoint my older brother Arthur Peter Davies as the sole executor of my estate . . . (*His voice fades down then up again*) . . . that the monies which I have placed in trust for my son Peter shall be made available to him in their entirety on his thirty-fifth birthday. Meanwhile, the fund is to be managed with all due diligence and invested at the sole discretion of this company's senior partner.

And last, that the series of recordings I have made for my said son Peter should be safely kept, together with the transcripts thereof, and delivered to him at the times specified.

SCENE 3 (1994)

Peter is coming home from work. As he opens the front door, his twelve-year-old son Tom accosts him.

Tom: Dad! There's a package for you.
Peter: Oh yes?
Tom: Open it, Dad. Go on.
Peter: Let me get in the door first.
Felicity: (*Kissing him*) Hello darling. Happy birthday.
Tom: Dad!
Peter: Yes all right, boy!
Tom: Oh go on, Dad.
Felicity: Ever since the postman came, he's been waiting for
    you to get home.
Tom: Who's it from, Dad? Is it a birthday present?
Peter: All right. All right! (*Peter opens the package.*)
Tom: What is it?
Peter: Funny, I was thinking about him today.
Felicity: What . . . ?
Peter: It's from the old man. I wondered if there were any more.
Tom: But what is it? What? What?
Felicity: Tell him, Peter.
Peter: Oh, Felicity, I don't know . . .
Felicity: He should know.
Tom: Tell me, Dad. Tell me.
Peter: One day.
Tom: You always say that.
Peter: Okay, Tom. Let's sit down.

SCENE 4 (1962)

Thomas's bedside. In the background we hear a hospital ward.
Arthur: Thomas, Thomas. It's Dr. Wilson, Thomas.
Thomas: (*Stirring*) What? Who is it? What did you say?
Arthur: The doctor, Thomas.

Thomas: Oh good.
Arthur: Good morning, doctor.
Dr. Wilson: Morning.
Arthur: I'll be outside if you need me.
Thomas: No, Arthur. I'd like you to stay.
Arthur: Yes, very well.
Thomas: Morning Doctor.
Dr. Wilson: Morning.
Thomas: How am I?
Dr. Wilson: How do you feel?
Thomas: I don't feel . . . not wonderful.
Dr. Wilson: That's understandable. You must have plenty of rest, and no exertion.
Thomas: Have you got the results? It was today, wasn't it?
Dr. Wilson: Yes.
Thomas: And?
Dr. Wilson: I'm going to increase the morphia, which should help with the pain.
Thomas: Oh no. Not more dope.
Arthur: Easy Thomas.
Thomas: Dr. Wilson, I have two questions for you, and I need straight answers.
Dr. Wilson: Yes, er . . . put like that. Yes, of course.
Thomas: Will I recover? And if not, how long?
Dr. Wilson: The tumour has grown very rapidly. There's very little chance of a remission I'm afraid.
Arthur: Is there any chance?
Thomas: Please answer, doctor. One has a right.
Dr. Wilson: Yes, certainly . . . er, no, almost no chance at all.
Thomas: I see. And how much time do you think?
Dr. Wilson: Well, that really is impossible to say. But it could be as little as a month, maybe less.
Thomas: Thank you, doctor. I appreciate your candour.
Dr. Wilson: Is there anything we can do? I mean is there anything you'd like? We'll certainly do our best to make you comfortable.

Thomas: Yes, I think there might be something. . . . Arthur, I'll need your help.

SCENE 5 (1994)

Peter, explaining to Tom.

Peter: You see Tom, my dad, your grandfather knew he was going to . . .
Tom: Going to what?
Peter: He was ill for . . . it must have been more than a year overall. I don't really remember. . . . I was a couple of years younger than you, Tom, when the first one came. He couldn't sing in tune, . . . but that didn't matter.

SCENE 6

Thomas's first letter. Faint and occasional sounds of a hospital ward.

Hello Peter,
This is Daddy speaking. I want to wish you a very happy birthday. I expect by now the others have all sung to you, and now I'm going to sing too.
Happy birthday to you,
Happy birthday to you,
Happy birthday dear Peter,
Happy birthday to you.
Three cheers for Peter. Hip pip hooray. Hip pip hooray. Hip pip hooray!
It's the end of September 1962, and I'm sitting very comfortably in the hospital garden. It's . . . er . . . well, there's a tree—it's a beech—and a lawn where I am. Quite a large one, almost big enough for a cricket pitch I think. And behind me the hospital building—big, Victorian, covered in ivy. And there's a clematis with a single purple bloom on it. It's a late one. On the other side of the grass are some rhodo-

dendrons. No flowers on them this time of year of course. Arthur has set me up with everything I need. It is a warm afternoon, there is a gentle breeze. Perhaps you will hear the birdsong. I seem to have the place to myself. No one comes here much.

It is surprising to be able to speak these word to you now, at the end of September 1962, and know that they will reach you in February 1963. No different from posting a letter, I suppose.

Well, my dear boy, I wish you to be happy at all times, but especially today on your birthday. So, now you're eleven! Well that's a good age to be. You'll be doing quite a lot of growing up in the next few years, but take my advice and don't be in too much of a hurry about it. It will all take care of itself in due course. There's still plenty of time for playing football and riding bicycles and for a newspaper comic every now and then.

When I was your age I had a particular fondness for a sweet called Gobstopper. I have to say that my daddy didn't really approve of my eating them, and I took care that he should never see me with one. You know, I am sure he would have enjoyed them as well as I—he did have rather a sweet tooth—but he thought the word—Gobstopper—rather vulgar. They cost four for a farthing and I remember buying them from old Mr. Hunter at the corner shop. He had a white moustache and he smoked a pipe—I thought he must be about a hundred years old. Anyway, the point is, I've asked Uncle Arthur to give you a large bag of Gobstoppers today, er, from me. I hope you like them.

February the twenty-fifth. A good date to be born on! The winter is coming to an end, perhaps you've had one or two fine days already. It will soon be spring.

All my life I loved the spring. When I was a boy, I used to think you could eat the cherry blossom, if you knew how to. I particularly loved the colours of the spring, the fresh greens, and all the spring flowers. A good gardener once told me that there's no such thing as a bad composition in nature. Whatever flowers and plants grow next to each other, the colours never clash. I think he was right. In any event, I've never caught it out.

It seems to me that the spring gives us hope for the whole year. When, in due course, the glories of the summer and the autumn have faded as they must and everything seems to perish at the year's end, we have to remember that there must be a winter so that there can be another spring!

Well, I shan't ramble on for long, but I do want to say one or two things more, so please listen patiently and forgive me if I sound solemn.

I must admit, when I was eleven years old I thought that all adults were very serious. The strange thing is, Peter, even now at my advanced age of forty-two, I still think that a bit. Even though I've been a grown man for quite a long time now, part of me is still that eleven-year-old boy who wanted to laugh at times when the grown-ups would have diapproved. But then, laughter and tears are often two sides of the same coin.

You may have been sad at times in these recent months. If so, don't worry, that's quite to be expected and in time the sadness will pass away. The great rule with this sort of thing is to face it bravely. I don't mean putting a brave face on it, or anything like that. I just mean be brave enough to be sad if you want to, cry if you want to, and then—and this is important—be brave enough not to be sad anymore when the sadness has gone. I hope that makes some sort of sense.

It's nearly spring, the time when everything in the world is trying to grow up. Well old chap, that's what you have to do now. So I want you to work hard at school, do all your homework, and take care of Mummy for me, as I know she will take care of you.

Always do your best Peter, and if it's your very best, you shan't go far wrong in life. For my part, I promise to watch over you as best I may, and if you ever need me, well, I shan't be able to talk to you face to face, but perhaps I shall be nearer than we can know.

Your Uncle Arthur is your godfather as well as your uncle, and he will watch over you too and be able to help you in ways which I cannot.

Happy birthday again, Peter.

Scene 7 (1994)

Peter, Tom, and Felicity.

Tom: He sounds old-fashioned.

Peter: Yes, he does.

Tom: Like in one of those black and white films on the telly.

Felicity: (*Laughing*) Oh Tom!

Tom: He does.

Felicity: I know darling. But he . . . he doesn't sound like that on the other ones, not so much. I think it's because he was trying—you say Pete.

Peter: What Mum means is that he was trying to be proper. Trying to sound like, for example, a voice he'd heard reading the news on the radio.

Tom: Why?

Felicity: Because he thought that was the way it was done.

Peter: Also, it was a difficult thing for him to do.

Tom: People make recordings all the time.

Peter: Yes. No. Not like that. Suppose you and I could never talk to each other again. Suppose all we could do was leave messages for each other.

Tom: Oh.

Felicity: Play the next one.

Peter: Do you want to hear the next one?

Tom: Yes. Definitely.

Peter: All right, I'm going to get a glass of wine first. Felicity?
Felicity: Yes please.
Tom: Can I have one?
Peter: Wine?
Tom: Oh go on. You always say I'm too young. Go on.
Peter: Tom, drink whatever you want today.

SCENE 8 (1962)

The hospital garden. An afternoon in September. Birds and distant traffic in the background.

Arthur: What about Bach?
Thomas: No, Mozart first. It's all downhill after that.
Arthur: And Shakespeare?
Thomas: Yes. But comedy before tragedy.
Arthur: Wine before beer?
Thomas: Cocktails at the Savoy!
Arthur: (*Laughing*) Ah yes!
Thomas: (*Laughing*) Remember? How squiffy we used to get!
Arthur: Of course!
Thomas: It's good to get out. Good idea Arthur.
Arthur: Better than in the ward. I think it might upset some
    of the others.
Thomas: Good of you to lug all this equipment about. Do
    you think it'll pick up the birds singing?
Arthur: I suppose it might. That'd be rather nice, perhaps?
Thomas: Yes. What about the traffic?
Arthur: It's quite faint.
Thomas: Mmm . . . Galleries, of course.
Arthur: Certainly. The Louvre.
Thomas: The Tate. The Turners!
Arthur: Fishing?
Thomas: Of course, and the Trout Inn—obviously.

Arthur: First catch first.

Thomas: Pawn to king four.

Arthur: Pawn to queen's knight three.

Thomas: Best attack is defense.

Arthur: Moorland.

Thomas: Or Ireland even.

Arthur: The Hebrides?

Thomas: Ah . . . no, no save that. Fine garden, this.

Arthur: Yes.

Thomas: I'd love to see that rhododendron over there in bloom.

Arthur: Perhaps we should get started.

Thomas: All set?

Arthur: Say when.

Thomas: Let's go.

SCENE 9

The second letter. Sounds of the garden.

Hello Peter,

Sixteen years is a threshold birthday. It may not seem like it now, but believe me, it is so. I wonder what you think about all the changes and developments that have been happening to you recently?

Thinking back to myself at that time, I realise that it was only later that I understood its potentials. Would you agree that one's powers are in an almost inspirational state? Certainly physically (you may not be as strong as you'll ever be now but you've certainly got as much energy as you'll ever have), if you develop some athletic skills now, they will stand you in good stead all your life. Intellectually this is a time of huge capacity. Even emotionally, which I think is the slowest faculty to grow up, isn't it fair to say that at this time one's feeling responses are characterised by great idealism.

But it's not for me to tell you what it's like for you. I only know what it was like for me.

I was sixteen when I first became serious about the law. It was an obvious choice—my father was a barrister and Arthur had already decided to take the same route. It began with a conversation I had with my father. I wasn't until then very close to him. I think respect is the word that applies most nearly to what I thought and felt about him. He always seemed to be too busy to bother with his sons. I mustn't be too hard on him; he was the nearest thing I ever knew to a man of perfect integrity, and he instilled in me a regime of effort and hard work which in later years saved me and made me. He also gave me my two great pastimes. Fishing was one, and chess the other.

At any rate, when I was sixteen, he called for me after supper. I had the same feeling going to the appointment—for such it was—as when in later years I had to face a rather unsympathetic bank manager. In short, I was frightened. I thought he was going to tear me off a strip for not studying hard enough or some such thing.

We sat by the fire in his study and to my great surprise he offered me a whisky, which I accepted. He started to talk about his career. He told me about his early days, the difficulties he faced in getting started, his first important case, how his fortunes had changed after that, what it was to run a practise.

I was fascinated. I'd never heard any of it before—he kept his business life quite separate from his family one. After a while he began to speak about what law, or "The Law" (as he called it) had meant to him. He said it was something to live one's life by, and that the foundation of it was honesty and plain dealing, and if one could hold to that in one's daily life one would find there was room for compassion also, and maybe later even the beginnings of wisdom. He said he loved The Law because it made civilisation possible and that he believed that at some level all who practised it longed for Justice to prevail even though appearances and ignorant men sometimes failed this high aspiration.

Listening to him I was inspired. He was talking about ideals—how things should be, could be he believed if only we all played our part. At length, he asked me if I'd given any thought to what I would do when my schooling came to an end. I said at once that I'd like to follow him and practise law as well. He smiled at me and I think he was very touched. Still smiling, he got up and poured us each another whisky.

He said he'd noticed that I'd been doing well at school, which was good, lawyers needed quick wits. He said not to neglect my Latin—I grimaced, it was the only subject I really disliked, but he said if one wanted to achieve anything one had to learn to overcome likes and dislikes. And he smiled and laughed. I don't know why, but I laughed as well. We both laughed for over a minute I think, forgetting what was funny. We laughed for pleasure.

Then we sat for a while in silence, sipping our whisky and looking at the fire. I decided then and there that I would overcome my hatred of Latin if that's what it took to be a lawyer. I know now that it was with the thought of pleasing him. Given the man he was, one could have worse foundations for a career.

"Thomas," he said.

I said, "Yes Father." I always called him Father—boys did in those days.

"Thomas, we're going to have a year together, you and I. Every week we'll do something together. Every Friday or Saturday, just you and I. The Law is a marvellous thing, but it can be as dry as dust if it's all you have. So don't decide anything finally tonight. After all, there are lots of other things in life and this may not be for you. We'll have a year."

I went to bed that night wildly excited. I thought I should be a fine barrister, maybe one day king's counsel (as it was then). But in fact my elation was because I had a new friend—my father.

The next year was truly a feast of riches. He never told me where we were going. The day before he'd leave a note saying, "Evening dress tomorrow" or "Something comfortable," or "Pack for the country." We went to the theatre, the opera, to concerts, to ballet, to art galleries, sometimes to diner where he would talk about wine. In the summer he taught me to fish, and once we had four entire days in the Yorkshire moors. We ate bread and cheese and took long walks, in the evenings we talked over chess. It was to have been a week, but he was called back to town by telegram. He said I could travel with him or stay out the week and make my own way back. I said I'd stay, and could see he was pleased. It would be an adventure to be alone in the wilds for a boy unused to it. He always looked for courage in me. That was my first real experience of solitude.

It was the year I . . . I cannot say that I got to know him, I never did that. It was the year I approached him. We did become close, and even though there was always an element of reserve in our relationship, at the time I thought I understood his life. Much later on, I realised that I knew about him only what he chose to tell me.

At the end of the year, he drew it to a close quite formally. He was a very formal man. We sat in his study again, again sipping whisky, and he asked me if I had made a decision. I said that I had decided I would study law. He clapped me on the shoulder, raised his glass and said, "Here's to it then, Thomas. I'm pleased."

I have to tell you, Peter, that year has stayed with me always. Now, at last, I saw my father as a man, not the austere and distant presence he had been until then. I realised that he was of his time, doing his best.

I gave him a present that night. One of his great loves was good wine and he could talk for hours about it. It was the only time I found him less than riveting—anyway, there was a particular Bordeaux which he had had once, and I managed to track down a bottle of it, and even pay for it myself. After he toasted me, I gave it to him. When he saw what it was, he took it in delight.

"How on earth did you find this? Thomas, I hadn't looked for this. Thank you my boy. Let this be a rule in your life. Always give, Thomas, when you can, always give."

It's good advice, and I'm passing it on to you. What your grandfather didn't tell me then but what I discovered later is that if you give yourself, others will give to you. I think that is The Law.

What I should like to give you now is a year like grandfather gave to me. I can't be there myself. Arthur will take my place. Enjoy the year, Peter, and again happy birthday.

Scene 10 (1994)

Peter, Tom, and Felicity.

Tom: Arthur?

Felicity: Uncle Arthur. Nice man.

Peter: Yes. Lovely man.

Tom: So did you have that year together?

Peter: Up to a point.

Tom: What do you mean?

Peter: Oh . . . it's difficult to explain. You see, Tom, I didn't really want it.

Tom: Why not?

Peter: Because . . . I was angry about it. I mean I knew for sure that I didn't want to be a barrister, and I didn't want him telling him how to do things, how to live . . .

Tom: He wasn't.

Felicity: No, but it seemed like it at the time.

Peter: See, Tom, I felt cheated. Cheated out of a father . . . and . . . of course, I don't feel like this now, but I was so angry with him.

Tom: What for?

Peter: For dying. For not being there.

Tom: But it wasn't his fault.

Peter: I know it wasn't. Anyway, I did go to dinner with Arthur a few times. It was nice, he was very fond of me, but he had the sense to let me go my own way.

Felicity: Arthur told me that he was afraid of trying to replace your father.

Peter: That's right, that's why he kept his distance.

SCENE 11 (1962)

The hospital garden. Some birdsong.

Thomas: I think it might rain.

Arthur: It might. But then again . . .

Together: It might not!

Arthur: Are you warm enough?

Thomas: Yes. The blanket's fine.

Arthur: I'll switch it on shall I? Ready?

Thomas: But didn't you bring—you didn't forget?

Arthur: No, of course not. I've got it here in my bag.

Thomas: Well done. Come on then.

Arthur: I just wonder if it's such a good idea, Thomas. I mean normally of course, but what with the morphia and so forth . . .

Thomas: Oh, I've been chucking most of that down the sink anyway. It'll be fine.

Arthur: Let's do the recording first. Then, maybe, afterward.

Thomas: No, I won't want it afterward. We'll drink to him now.
Arthur: All right. I'll keep the bottle in my bag. Use the cups
    from your thermos—don't let anyone see. . . . What is it?
Thomas: (*Chuckling*) I was just thinking, that night—I've
    never been so cold since.
Arthur: Should think not. Right then. Cheers.
Thomas: Cheers.

SCENE 12

The third letter. Garden background.

Happy birthday, Peter,

Oh my dear boy. How I wish I could be with you on this
day. I can't bear it that I can't.

No. Of course I can bear it. I must.

The truth is, I'm just a little bit plastered, not to put too fine
a point on it. Arthur managed to smuggle in a bottle of champagne. Against regulations here of course, goes without
saying. But bless your uncle. I told him. I said, "If I'm going to talk to my boy on his twenty-first, I'm going to need
champagne. And it's gone down rather well I must say.

On my twenty-first, I did a silly thing. I had some leave,
I came back from Sullum Voe, I was stationed up there . . .
there was a bit of a mix up with an old girlfriend and a
chap from the RAF—oh Peter, don't ever be a flyer. At any
rate, what with one thing and another, I ended up swim-
ming naked in the Serpentine at midnight. Oh! It was cold!

Not such a bright caper. But there are times when you've
just got to do these things. Bear in mind that we all behaved
oddly given the circumstances. I hadn't seen action yet, but
the chance of it was always there. I've sometimes wondered
what I would have been like if I hadn't been through it. I
think we get the answers to that sort of question at the end
of our time, in which case I shall soon know.

Pause.

Oh. That's a bit maudlin isn't it?

Alcohol you see is a great changer of mood. Perhaps the best use of it is to strengthen one's fancy. Yes! It's fair to say that nicely tight one can have ideas which simply may not be available in sobriety. I can't think of any just now. It's a fine anaesthetic too—if a temporary one merely. Not for physical pain. No. There is no pain to match the pain of lost potential. Unlived life.

All that aside, what I want to say today is . . . it's a day to celebrate. Which is why we've set aside a magnum of Dom Perignon—I wanted Arthur to drink it with you himself— but he said by this time you'd have your own friends and be wanting their company more than his, or mine come to that—I'm sure he's wise.

No advice either, this is the time for you to make your own discoveries, but there is one theme and flavour of the time which sticks in my mind. Comradeship. Friendship. Some friendships made then have lasted until now, some have been lost. It was my privilege to have Arthur as my big brother—he's always looked out for me. I hope you are blessed with such a friend. And so, on this day when you progress further into your life's spring, think of me not as one who walks with you, but as one standing on the side-lines yelling encouragement and raising a glass of bubbly, as I do now this moment (*he drinks*) to wish you health, wealth, and happiness.

Happy birthday, lad.

Your just now inebriated father.

SCENE 13 (1994)

Peter, Tom, and Felicity.

Tom: Have you ever been drunk, Dad?

Peter: Oh, once or twice.

Tom: Have you, Mum?

Felicity: Once or twice.

Tom: Can we all get drunk together?

Peter: What, now?

Tom: No, sometime.

Peter: Sure, we'll give you champagne for your twenty-first.

SCENE 14 (1962)

The hospital boiler room. The sound of pipes gurgling.

Arthur: It's like being in a submarine. All these pipes. There. All set. I'm getting quite good at all this technical stuff.

Thomas: If that bloody boiler goes off, we're sunk—no pun intended.

Arthur: No, no. We'll just switch off, rewind, and do it again. Are you expecting it to go off?

Thomas: Apparently it's meant to fire up every thirty minutes, but the maintenance chap told me it's got a mind of its own.

Arthur: Let's get on then.

The door opens, Sister comes in.

Sister: Mister Davies! What an earth is going on here?

Thomas: Ah Sister, hello. You see it's raining outside, so we've just popped in here. We're recording you see.

Sister: Quite apart from the irregularity, it's filthy. I'm afraid I couldn't possibly allow—

Arthur: Sister, I wonder if I could just have a quick word with you outside?

Sister: Who are you?

Arthur: I'm Mister Davies's brother. Also Mister Davies. Arthur. Arthur Davies.

Sister: And would you care to explain what's going on here?

Arthur: Certainly Sister. It's a particular situation actually. Shall we just pop outside? Or into your office might be best.

Sister: It's no use trying to smile your way around me.

Arthur: Good heavens no, Sister. I wouldn't dream of it. But I'd take it very kindly if you—

Sister: Oh, very well. It had better be convincing.

Arthur: Yes indeed. Thomas, why don't you get started? Shan't be long.

SCENE 15

The fourth letter. Boiler room background.

Hello Peter, and happy birthday,

I hope it is a happy day. I hope that, because I can honestly say that the year following my twenty-ninth birthday was the most difficult in my life so far. That is why I have chosen this time to talk to you again.

There's no reason why it should be as troublesome a time for you, but it does seem as if nearly everyone experiences extremes of difficulty at some time or other in this life. Maybe you have already faced such a time—if so, then you will be better placed than before to understand the sufferings of others. If not, my story may be of interest and possibly even of use should you find yourself in similar circumstances one day.

The war was four years finished. I had completed my studies. I returned to Oxford—places were held for those of us who left to fight. It was hard to become a student again, I had lost the relish for it, that keen inspiration planted by my father which had made it easy to study before. Neither could I enjoy student company. They all seemed so flippant to me.

However, I persevered—more through lack of an alternative than anything else.

When I came down to London, I took a bedsitting room in South Kensington. I had not managed to arrange anything in the way of a job while up at Oxford, and I could not bring myself to look for one. I had a few hundred pounds left—quite a lot of money then.

For a little while I followed a routine. I rose early and took a walk in Kensington Park Gardens. I tried to continue a regime of study, and in the mornings I would go to the Kensington library, after lunch I visited the museums or the galleries. But I couldn't bear people, I preferred loneliness.

One morning at the end of the summer of 1949 I gave it up. Just that.

I woke early as usual, but when I looked for a reason to get up, there wasn't one. I tried to will myself awake, but there was just no purpose in it. I closed my eyes and slept until past noon. The whole of the following week, I scarcely moved. I did not shave or wash, ate at random. The week became two, and then just a succession of days. All structure went out of my life. For occupation I would wander the streets, sometimes not even that.

You see, for a long time I had lived by my father's code. After that, during the war it was the need of the time that carried us all along. Now I had to find a way to carry on that was my own. As I sank further into a depression, meaning in life seemed ever more distant.

It went on like that until the end of the year. Arthur had been trying to rally me. Finally, when at Christmas he insisted I come home with him for our parents' sake, I told him I didn't want to see him again, and to stay out of my affairs. For the first time I had cut myself off from my best friend.

By the beginning of 1950, I was teetering on the brink of serious mental illness. I began to experience fears and delusions. Where lethargy had kept me sleeping in bed before, now I was terrified at the way the man in the tobacconists would look at me when I bought ten Players, or in the glance of the woman at the tea house I would sense conspiracy. There were other symptoms too which I shan't trouble you with.

Later on, when I tried to make sense of this episode, I supposed it was the effect of the war. I had been conscious of no anguish at the time, and I was as exhilarated as anyone else when it finished. But there was trauma in those years, and many found it appalling to return to ordinary life as if nothing had happened.

This is the mystery of character, isn't it? The events themselves are neutral; the hazard is how we load them.

This was the time for me when I had to find myself. If not my Self directly—for that is a lifetime's search—then the beginnings of that finding. Reduced by circumstances until at last something within stands firm. Perhaps that's putting it too grandly.

It was the spring that saved me. At the end of March I saw through my window a tree perhaps a week into new leaf. I don't know how to describe the effect this simple sight had on me. I suppose the tree had been there all along, I had just not noticed it. With the sight of the new leaves, I knew that those black days could end if I chose it so. It was a dangerous moment, for I knew that I could also fail the choice. Suddenly I was in turmoil.

I made myself wash and shave, and that calmed me a little. Then, in better spirits than for many months, I went outside to take stock and think. I was now down to three pounds, enough money for about two weeks. As I turned toward Exhibition Road to walk up to the park, it came to me that there was no need to suffer a final decline, and that as long as I had strength in my arms I could work if there was work to be had. It was a wonderful feeling.

London was just starting to rebuild itself after the war damage. Within two days I found work as a labourer. The first week passed in a numbness of fatigue. With the first pay packet, I bought three pounds of steak, tossed it in a frying pan for ten minutes, and ate the lot in a single sitting, then slept the clock round.

It took quite a while for my body to get accustomed to the work—to begin with I would stagger home aching in all my muscles and collapse into sleep. My oversensitive, overactive mind was silenced by my body's exhaustion . . . as I remember, it wasn't until midsummer that I had any energy left over for thinking!

Physical work was the salve to my frazzled nerves, but the time also taught me valuable lessons. Many of the men on the sites were desperately hard up, it was easy to see how we can be tempted to misdeeds by grinding poverty. It was very useful to know this when later on, practising as a barrister and having experienced a little real adversity myself, I found there was room for the compassion which my father had spoken of when facing men damaged by their own folly.

I made it up with Arthur. Nothing much was said. There was no need. He understood. As so often he came quickly to my aid. When he saw that I was again in the land of the living, he arranged a position for me with his own firm.

At Arthur's suggestion, I took a walking holiday in the Hebrides. Ah, Peter, if ever your spirits need lifting, go there. Islands are magical places. The colours of the flowers—it must be the sea moisture in the atmosphere—are so brilliant, so vivid. And if you get silent enough, somewhere in some lonely spot, you might fancy you see the little people feasting in the mist. Yes, go there—but remember to take something against the midges!

Now I see that year—it was almost a calendar year—as a cycle of redemption. I am grateful that I fell no further than I did, though it was far enough. If you ever face some darkness of soul, I want to say to you, remember to hope. It was only when I found strength to hope that my circumstances improved. We talk of vicious circles, but I believe that hope can be the beginning of benevolent ones. So it was for me.

SCENE 16 (1994)

Tom, Peter, and Felicity.

Peter: Poor old Thomas.

Felicity: He came through it though.

Peter: Amazing really. Not much help around at that time.

Tom: When you were twenty-nine, were you as unhappy as he was?

Peter: Actually I was for a while. Funny. This was the first of the tapes that really made sense, because for the first time I was going through or I'd just been through something similar.

Tom: Like him?

Peter: Not exactly like. But this was the time when I finally accepted him—began to. For what he was.

Tom: How could you do that? He wasn't there.

Peter: I think we are all profoundly affected by who our fathers are. Even if they're absent. Maybe specially if they are.

Tom: Did you work on a building site?

Peter: No, but I did have a touch of that kind of depression, like he did.

Tom: How did you get better?

Peter: Talking. Just talking about it.

Tom: We're talking now.

Felicity: That's right.

Peter: Up till this one, the other tapes seemed to have got it wrong in a way. For example, when I was twenty-one, I did actually drink the champagne with Arthur.

Felicity: That's because he was engaged.
Tom: To Granny?
Peter: How did you know that?
Tom: It's obvious.
Peter: Yes. Not to them, unfortunately. They broke it off.
Tom: Why?
Peter: Arthur only spoke about it once.
Felicity: I didn't know that.
Peter: About six months before his stroke.
Felicity: What did he say?
Peter: He told me that the trouble was . . . that he and Elaine—he and my mother—began to have this intense attraction to each other when Dad was ill. The problem was that Arthur and Dad never spoke about it openly.
Felicity: They must have.
Peter: Apparently not. I mean it took them ten years after Dad's death to get as far as being engaged. I think they just never managed to sort out what was grief, what was guilt.

SCENE 17 (1962)

The hospital garden. Birdsong.

Thomas: I never saw a clematis flowering in October.
Arthur: Yes. It's a late one.
Thomas: Arthur, I love these days.
Arthur: Yes. Cold, sharp, very clear.
Thomas: I didn't mean the weather. I meant—these days.
Arthur: Me too.
Thomas: It's the sort of time about which you'd say, "I'll always remember this."
Arthur: I know.
Thomas: What do you think? Is there anything after?

Arthur: You know, Tom, I must admit that I've never questioned that there is. Until recently. Recently I've wondered a great deal.

Thomas: And what . . . ?

Arthur: How can any of us say? There is no proof, after all.

Thomas: The trouble is . . . I find I don't want to go—I don't want to . . . it's not fair . . .

Arthur: Thomas! Stop it!

Thomas: I'm sorry.

Arthur: Do you think any of us want you to go? Elaine, or the boy, or me? Do you?

Thomas: Don't, Arthur.

Arthur: Of course it's not fair. It's not. But we're all going to—that is about the only sure thing there is.

Thomas: All right, Arthur! Now you stop it.

Arthur: Truce?

Thomas: Truce.

Arthur: Sure you're up to this today? We could leave it a day or two.

Thomas: No. I'll enjoy this one. Got any more of that coffee?

Arthur: Yes, I think so.

Thomas: Black, three sugars.

Arthur: But you hate sugar.

Thomas: I know.

SCENE 18

The fifth letter. Garden background.

My dear Peter,

You're thirty-five today! The summertime of your life. I wonder now, as with all these letters of mine, how your life is proceeding. And I hope as always that you are in the best possible health and fortune.

The gist of my letter this time is—at least I certainly hope it is—good news. As you know, I was lucky enough to be able to make some provision for your mother when I died (well, I'm not technically dead at this moment, but by the time you hear this . . . you know what I mean). It was a solace to me to know that she was provided for.

What you don't know is that I also made some provision for you. It was a complicated arrangement, involving trusts and so forth—complicated because I didn't want you to know about it. Arthur can give details if you're interested. You may wonder why I have waited until now, and you may be thinking that you could well have done with some cash a little sooner. I did give it some thought and concluded as follows:

Given that you are my son, there is a good chance that you will resemble me in character as well as in feature. Indeed, people already tell me that we look alike—I can't see it myself. I think you take after your mother's good looks rather than my plain ones.

It's been up to you to make something of the character you were given, but if, in fact, you are constituted a bit like me, then it wouldn't have done you any good to come into money earlier. What I'm saying is, I thought I knew it all when I was twenty-one. Ten years later I was beginning to understand that I didn't know much of anything. By the time I was your age, working day and night to support my family—that's when an inheritance would have been most useful to me.

If you have a family of your own by now, you'll already know two things. First, nothing anybody can say can prepare you for having children. Second, children, or as in my case a child, change everything in your outlook. In other words, at twenty-one I would have lived the life of Riley if I could have afforded to; at thirty-five . . . well, now it's up to you, isn't it?

When last I spoke to you it was all difficulty and dismay. Now it's more hopeful. Now I expect you'll have a profession.

Now is the time to work harder than ever before. You're coming into your best years. The Romans said a man's prime was from years thirty-five to fifty. Men are boys before that. Physically you may not have the stamina you had ten years ago, but now you have the vision. You know what to do. It says in the Bible, "Whatever is given thee to do; that do with all thy strength."

Childhood ends a long time after growing up. Sometime now, or in one of these years soon, I predict that you'll have a new sense of yourself. Let me put it this way: It is the beginning of your life's summer now. The time of flowers and fruit. After all, look at the plant life. I've often thought if people behaved like flowers in bloom they'd be arrested. Whatever it is you're up to Peter, give it everything you've got.

As ever, your father.

SCENE 19 (1994)

Tom, Peter, and Felicity.

Peter: Remember when we went to Hawaii?
Tom: 'Course. Was that what you did with the money?
Peter: There wasn't any money.
Felicity: When Arthur died, the firm changed hands. After that it went bust, and all the investments were lost.
Peter: So we took out another credit card and had a great time.
Felicity: We called it "Grandad's provision."
Peter: We thought he'd like that.
Felicity: There's a saying, Tom: "One generation makes it, the next uses it, the third loses it." Well, it's our turn to make it!
Tom: Okay.

Peter: Which brings us to this one. Shall I play it?
Tom: Yes.
Peter: More wine?
Tom: Yes.

SCENE 20

The last letter.

Hello Peter.

It's me again. I say again because it's only a few days since I recorded your thirty-fifth birthday letter. But if everything has gone according to plan, for you it will have been seven years since you heard it.

This is the last one.

No more after this. I'm forty-two years old, and if, as I dearly hope, you have lived this long, today is your forty-second birthday. So now we are the same age. Equal now in years and experience, and I'm sure you are as much a man as I was; at least as much.

So now, let us talk as old friends. I picture us sitting together at the Trout Inn at one of those tables by the stream. Did you visit it with Arthur? Perhaps it's a warm summer's evening, and we have some beer. There is a scent of honeysuckle, and the stream gurgles behind our talk.

When first I fell ill—rather, when I understood at last that it was terminal, that was about five weeks ago now—I had all sorts of powerful and disturbing feelings. At the outset, I was furious. What a sour trick of God, or fate, or whatever—after all, I might have been taken in the war as so many were. But having survived all that—after so long struggling away and at last building up some sort of career and reputation—not having to work quite so desperately hard . . . ah well.

As the illness has progressed, I have come to something close to acceptance.

In terms of grief, I was the lucky one. I had a chance to do my grieving beforehand. Life is very sweet when you face the loss of it. And you see, you may have lost me, but I also lost you.

To consider the implications for you was, I confess, a shattering experience. In the back of my mind I had all sorts of plans for you, and was looking forward to the ways in which I might encourage your interests and offer you things which I had enjoyed—and then I realised that parenthood is inevitably heartbreaking in the sense that you cannot give your children what you wish to give them because you are not what you wish to be. I think that is always true—how can it be otherwise—temperament aside, the distance of the years places us at odds. But how true now, now that I wished to live and could not.

In the dark days between the knowledge and the acceptance, I experienced what I can only call torrents of feeling. Your mother once said, Elaine once said, "When you have children, you love more than you knew you had love in you."

The battle of life, so to speak, makes it at first possible, at length, all too easy to forget that. But the prospect of loss brings it all sharply into full relief. We decided, Elaine and I, your mother and I, rightly or wrongly, not to tell you that I would most likely die—after all, you would know it soon enough.

There was a morning last spring when I was watching you playing in your tree house. You didn't see me looking at you through the study window. I wanted to run to you and hug you in my arms and tell you never to forget me and that I would always love you no matter what happened. No matter what you did in life, good or bad. No matter if you were a great success or a spectacular failure or something in-between. No matter even if you never cared for me or thought of me—that I would always love you just because you existed and because—the glory of it—you were my son.

I didn't do it of course; perhaps I should have. But I had little practise in showing my feelings, and I thought I might frighten you.

This whole area of feelings, I've never been good at it. Isn't that silly? To have lived forty-two years, and not know how to say, "I love you." Largely my upbringing I suppose. We were taught that it was girlish to show feelings, and that boys didn't cry, and many more things of that sort.

Scene 21 (1962)

The hospital. A private room. Arthur switches off the recorder.

Arthur: Thomas. Thomas, are you all right?

Thomas: Yes, I'm fine. I'll be fine. Just taking a little breather.

Arthur: Look, shall we call it a day?

Thomas: No, no. No. I want to finish it today. It's all right. It'll be a great relief to get it done.

Arthur: Do you want another pillow?

Thomas: Yes, good idea. Prop me up. You've always done that Arthur.

Arthur: Rubbish! How's that?

Thomas: Much better. Right. Before we go on . . .

Arthur: Yes?

Thomas: Thank you, Arthur. For everything. Thank you so much.

Arthur: Great privilege, Thomas.

Thomas: You must look after them for me.

Arthur: Of course. I'll . . . I will.

Thomas: I know you will. Peter . . . he's so young . . .

Arthur: He'll mend.

Thomas: I wonder. I wonder if that's the point, in a way. But Elaine—

Arthur: She's a very strong person.

Thomas: Arthur.

Arthur: Thomas.

Thomas: I don't know why this is difficult to say.

Arthur: You needn't say anything . . .

Thomas: No. But I . . . (*chuckles*).

Arthur: What?

Thomas: I'll more regret what I don't say I think. If there's ever anyone else for her—

Arthur: Elaine?

Thomas: You know . . . the right sort.

Arthur: Yes?

Thomas: Encourage her Arthur, will you?

Arthur: Yes Thomas. Yes.

Thomas: Got those pills handy?

Arthur: Here they are.

Thomas: No, I'll have them afterward. I did without last night too. I want to be lucid.

Arthur: Right.

Thomas: Why have they given me my own room?

Arthur: Ah well, that was me. I explained to Sister there was only one more. She told them to put you in here. Said you might as well stay—oh my God!

Thomas: Direct type, Sister. Blunt even.

Arthur: Thomas, I'm sorry.

Thomas: Why? Don't be. It's no surprise. I know we're nearly finished. Should we go back to the beginning?

Arthur: No, no. I just rewind to where you left off, and we start from there. No one listening to it would ever know we've been chatting. Got the notes?

Thomas: Yes. Here. Where was I?

Arthur: Feeling. You were talking about feeling.

    Arthur switches the recorder on.

SCENE 22

The final part of the last letter.

During the war, there was a lot of feeling around, but that was different. We had a great purpose. In extremis we would have given our lives for a comrade—how many did so. There was unity on the streets and in the battlefields. The brutality of it was hideous though—and the absurdity! Loss, waste, destruction, on a vast scale . . .

But I remember sensing acutely the day after the war ended that the phoenix which had risen from these ashes of carnage—that Being which had made possible efforts beyond the limits of strength, unlooked-for courage, great sacrifice; and which had found its highest expression in the love which serves the highest purpose—that this same phoenix would fade again, and once more seem lost, as it does now.

Perhaps this is the rule. At times of threshold and crisis we have our greatest opportunities. It certainly seems so now that my personal battle is almost over.

So . . . I have sent you these letters at times in you life which I guessed were important ones. I've had only my own life to go on of course, knowing nothing of the challenges which you have faced or what strengths they called forth in you. I decided that the messages should come irregularly over the years. I wanted you to know something about me, but I did not want to be too often talking to you. Your fate has decreed that you grew up without a father. One of the advantages of that is that your mistakes, your successes, are your own at least. You stand in no one's shadow. I've never been a religious person, but I now believe that earthly fatherhood is a token really of that which fathers us all.

Peter, have you noticed how the passing of time accelerates as one gets older? In childhood a day can seem a year almost, and a season becomes almost a state of being. Those long summer holidays packed with incident and adventure. Maybe it's because as each year passes a year becomes a smaller fraction of one's total life so far. How then to explain the connections between experiences far separated from each other in the sequence from birth to death? Our lives are not linear in that regard, but cyclic. Whatever the explanation, the whole thing speeds up for sure. This last year for me has flashed by. If that continues, then in a few minutes now you will be eighty. And when you die—as all who live must do—then we shall meet again.

I am aware now that these messages of mine may well seem more and more dated as each one is delivered. Aware too of how much is left unsaid, and that a father's last thoughts are a pale substitute for the real thing. Forgive me for that; you see, at this pass this is the best I can do.

Bless you my boy. My dear friend, my son. I wish you happiness in all things.

I love you, Peter.

I know now that love is the key. I wish I had known it sooner.

Farewell.

SCENE 23 (1994)

Peter, Tom, and Felicity.

Peter: So . . . that was the old man. He was right about one thing—if I'd inherited money when I was twenty-one I'd have blown it.

Felicity: He got other things right too.

Peter: How?

Felicity: Well, he loved you.

Peter: Yes.

Tom: But the money never came, and you didn't have that

year with Uncle Arthur, so he didn't really leave you anything.

Peter: But I did get the champagne when I was twenty-one.

Felicity: You've always had a taste for it since.

Peter: True! You see, Tom, my life hasn't gone like his, and he couldn't live it for me—he knew that. But he did leave me something. He left the best thing.

Tom: What?

Peter: He left himself. Just himself.

Tom: Are you all right Dad?

Peter: I'm fine.

Tom: Am I called Tom after him?

Peter: Yes, you are. Tom. Give me a hug, Tom.

Tom: Happy birthday Dad.

SCENE 24 (1962)

Thomas's bedside.

Arthur: We've finished, Tom. It was a great effort.

Thomas: Yes, it was.

Arthur: I'll make all the arrangements.

Thomas: Will he understand? Will he get it?

Arthur: As you've said yourself, that's for him.

Thomas: Yes. Our lives are our own. Alone.

Arthur: But we can hold hands along the way.

Thomas: Hold my hand now Arthur.

Arthur: Here, Thomas.

SCENE 25

Tom's diary.

Tom: 26th February 1994. It was Dad's birthday yesterday. It was a good one I think. Why didn't he tell me about it before? I suppose he thought I was too young. But it's my story as well as his. After all, I am his son.

It's funny to hear Grandfather's voice. He sounded like a stranger. But this stranger was my father's father, and I am related to him too. I feel as if I knew him a bit. I liked him.

Dad laughed when I gave him his present after supper. It was a good idea to buy him a bottle of wine.

The House Sitter

The House Sitter

"It's a provocative statement," mused Benedict, "but I think its a true one."

He had just finished telling me in detail about some deal which would net him a substantial profit. It was a story involving backhanders and sweeteners. So used had he become to this kind of thing that he no longer noticed any risk to his integrity.

"What is a provocative statement?" I asked.

"One's Being attracts one's life."

I remembered his face as it had been those passionate times years ago, when we were poor, and young, and aspiring, and had sworn eternal friendship. Where was that face now? At that moment an idea stole upon my mind and I gasped at the scope of it. "I mean look at me," droned Benedict, "rich, successful, surrounded by possessions that I'm sure I don't remotely need. But am I happy? Whereas you, Giles, oh I do admire your courage . . ."

"You'll miss your flight," I said. "They've called it twice." I escorted Benedict to the security barrier. "Leave everything with me," I smiled, "You need a really good holiday, see you in two weeks."

Cruising at speed in Benedict's Mercedes, I reviewed the plan which had come to me. Yes, it seemed possible. I found myself reflecting upon him, and the great change which was about to come into his life. I had known him since university days. He had studied Law, I had read English. Throughout the fifteen years since, he had kept me on his dinner-party list as the token Bohemian, once confessing to me that he always counted on me to either insult someone or attempt seduction, and therefore my novelty factor was high. We had communicated by phone too, he calling me to announce some new commercial flair which made him richer or to commiserate with some artistic failure of mine. Now, pushing forty, Benedict had it all. Very highly paid work in company law, romance on tap—he never permitted himself the distraction of commitment—but, above all, his beautifully appointed house in Chelsea which was the pride of his soul.

I had very little. He rang me and explained that he could save a thousand pounds on his insurance premiums if his house were occupied while he was on holiday, would I be interested in looking after the place? At the time of that phone call my address was a bed sitting room on the Blackhorse Road in Walthamstow, and my worldly goods amounted to a packet of Silk Cut and a word processor. Benedict would leave me with sufficient funds (in cash) to look after the running of the house, keep bills and staff paid, and a house sitter's fee. "No, no, no," I had protested feebly. "Yes, yes, yes," he had insisted. "Think of what I'm saving."

The idea of a fortnight's holiday in SW3 was attractive. Ah, the King's Road, where expensive people display their tasteful plumage and the cappuccino factor is high. I accepted his offer. Whilst he was relaxing in Bali, I would take luxury in Chelsea and soothe my frustrations.

But now something had happened that would change all that. What had happened was that in the moment when Benedict had visited his smug satisfaction at my failure upon me, an ecstacy of rage had swept through my body and created a resolve in me. I glided the state-of-the-art motorcar to a halt outside Benedict's house, parking heedlessly on a double yellow line. I unlocked the two Banhams, the one Chubb, the Yale, and pressed the code into the alarm keypad. I spent a merry half hour at the kitchen table roughing out a plan of events. I then went directly to the telephone, and by agreeing to pay three times the going rate because I had missed that week's deadline, managed to place advertisements with the *Kensington News & Post*, the *Fulham Chronicle*, the *Hampstead & Highgate Express*, and *LOOT*. It would be two days before the adverts came to press, but that would give me time to handle some of the more exclusive items and fine tune the arrangements for the rest of the project.

I went all over the house from basement to loft. I complimented Benedict on his taste, noticing for the first time, although I knew the house well, many details of care and expense—the mixer taps from Villeroy & Boch in each of the bathrooms, for example. There was a collection of vintage wines and ports in the cellar. I wondered if not having a licence would present a problem, and then laughed at my naivete—everything would be transacted in cash, and I was confident that people would pay top dollar.

I placed calls to a fine art dealer in Duke Street, Saint James, and an antiques dealer in New Bond Street. The following afternoon, after their visits to me, I had shipped out of the house a Georgian dining table with walnut inlays and matching chairs, a Venetian glass chandelier, and the seventeenth-century armoire in his bedroom. These items together with all the various paintings and prints—around thirty pieces, including a really beautiful Impressionist painting of the great ballerina Svetana—fetched me something approaching 50,000 pounds in cash, a modest proportion of their true value I know, but speed was the essential thing here. Benedict might not be planning to return for a full fortnight, but it would be best to have the thing completely wrapped up by then. It was now Thursday afternoon; one more thing to accomplished by the close of business. I rushed to Avis at Marble Arch and hired one of their transit vans. Then, satisfied with a terrific start to my plan, donned one of Benedict's linen suits and strolled down to the Four Seasons for a bowl of pasta and half a bottle of chianti, turning in at about 10:30.

I was glad of the early night because the following morning, Friday, I had a near disaster. Maria the cleaner was just letting herself in when I rushed to the door. "Didn't Mr Benedict inform you?" I demanded.

She said she knew that I was going to be staying here while he was away, but she still had to do her job. The best I could come up with was to say that I was working on a piece of performance art and needed complete solitude. I shoved three hundred pounds at her and that seemed to do the trick. Once she was safely gone, I started to load the van. Benedict had a taste for polished floorboard and rugs. There were fourteen in all and some of them quite heavy. I managed it finally, and drove to a carpet dealers in Hampstead. The rugs were Turkish and Chinese silks of the finest quality, as one would expect. The dealer's eyes were on stalks when I showed him what was inside the van; it was all the poor chap could do to come up with a lengthy monologue about markup and overheads. I was in a hurry.

"How much?"

"6,000 pounds," he whispered, expecting a rejection.

"Cash?" I asked. He nodded, and that was that.

Back to Chelsea where I bought a copy of the local paper and checked the advert. There it was: "Grand House Clearance Sale. Many luxury items at giveaway prices. Everything must go. Cash only. Friday, noon onward." Excellent!

I went to the telephone and booked an architectural salvage firm, a specialist timber yard, a plumber, and an electrician. I had just finished when the doorbell rang. There stood a neat bookish looking man. "Got any books?" he asked.

"About three thousand volumes."

"Hardback? Quality titles?"

"Yes."

"Grand, the lot?"

"Done!" I said. The neat man motioned to two youths standing on the pavement, and forty-five minutes later Benedict's house was empty of books. For good measure, I threw in his collection of old maps as well.

There was activity for the rest of the day, but between one and four was the most intense. After a hundred and fifty people I lost count, and was beginning to feel like a revolving door in a January sale. Kitchen appliances went first. Kettle, toaster, blender, the Le Creuset saucepans. The Wedgewood tea service. The Dartington Crystal wine glasses. The wine itself of course—silly to have been worried about that! But there was no method in it; people seemed determined to buy no matter what, and in very short time I sold everything that wasn't fixed down. Hoovers, iron, the stepladder. All the power tools in the cellar, the washing machine, the drier, dishwasher, the wall-mounted oven, the computer, two typewriters—I know that Benedict never used those so couldn't feel that he would miss them. Also, the obsolete record player languishing in the attic. The CD player from Bang and Olfsen had gone early along with the four televisions, each of which had digital stereo sound.

Midway through the afternoon the crisis came, and, though I say it myself, I was brilliant. Benedict's great hobby was the cultivation of Bonsai trees and he had something of a forest. I was getting rid of them at a tenner a throw, along with the bedding plants in the back garden, and, to my delight, the turf, when the lady next door stuck her head over the fence.

"I say," she trilled. "What's going on here?"

"Don't ask!" I shrilled back. "He's lost it my dear, but completely. Everything, everything cleared, and then—he wants the bedrooms Mediterranean, the lounge with Trompe l'Oeils à la Pompeii. The kitchen he insists is jet. And, can you believe it? He wants a jade bridge in the garden."

It just shows you how effective these house clearance adverts can be, because all through the following day, Saturday, I had people turning up asking me if there was anything left to buy. There simply wasn't, but one or two irate types didn't believe me and I had to let them pick their way through the men from architectural reclamation who were busy removing the fireplaces. They also managed to take down intact the ceiling roses which were original to the house, and the skirtings which were the really substantial ones you just don't see these days.

I had a tiny hiccup of timing, the plumber being delayed. I needed him to drain down the heating system and remove the radiators, as well as disconnect all the sinks, baths, and loos. But while we were waiting, I set the reclamation boys to work lifting the floorboards. Once the electrician and his team were in, going for all the fittings, the place really started to come apart. Even so, even with top-notch experienced tradespeople working flat out, it was fully the following Wednesday before the place was stripped back to the joists. Faster, I know, than it would have taken to build it.

I made a last pass through the building—you couldn't call it a house at that point. I had to go carefully, the stairs were still there, without the bannisters, but not the floors. I had left the plaster on the walls and ceilings (apart from the roses), there being no secondhand market in plaster. I had also left the Colefax & Fowler window fabrics at the front of the house just as they had been. I wanted to give the impression that nothing had changed while Benedict had been on holiday.

The results of my efforts were on the whole very satisfying. I had missed a couple of opportunities inevitably—the fired Earth kitchen tiles, I'm sure someone would have paid for the privilege of hacking those off—but on the whole I was pleased. I mean, I'd gone as far a selling the sash windows at the rear, and even toyed with the idea of dismantling the back walls and selling the bricks, but had rejected this, thinking it would have involved planning permission and all kinds of paperwork.

Financially, the thing had gone extremely well. I had over 130,000 pounds in cash, which just goes to show you what the contents of a house can be worth and how it doesn't do to be underinsured. Mind you, had I taken more time about it I obviously could have gotten a lot more—the fridge freezer, for example, I virtually gave away for eighty quid—but money wasn't the point.

I wrote Benedict a note. "Dear Benedict," I said. "I hope you had a really good holiday. I have been reflecting on our conversation at the airport, and I'm sure you were right—that stuff about you being surrounded by things you didn't really need. I think you'll find that's less of a problem now. There was something else too—oh yes, about *whom you are attracting to your life*. Welcome back to yours. Best wishes, Giles. P. S. I shan't be coming to dinner any more."

It was only then that I finally understood why I'd bothered. Anger? Yes. Also, envy, fury, rage. But in the end there was only one reason why I'd gone to these lengths. It was because I loved him. I felt, in this effort, I'd found a way to say symbolically, "Your spirit, friend, is more precious to me than gold." I thought of adding the phrase "I forgive you" to my note, but rejected this as patronising.

I pinned the note to the hall wall with a masonry nail, and stacked the parking tickets neatly beneath it. As I got into the Merc I looked back at Benedict's front door. I had locked the two Banhams, the one Chubb, the Yale. I couldn't set the alarm of course; that was no longer functioning. But it occurred to me as I drove away that it was all right to leave the place unalarmed because there was now nothing left to steal.

Something Frivolous

Something Frivolous

"FLORENCE," SAID RICHARD, as they sat at breakfast. "Florence, wasn't that a nice looking lady? The one who slapped that man's face in Selfridge's lift yesterday?"
Florence looked up from her cornflakes and regarded her father steadily. Richard returned her gaze. He hoped that his expression betrayed none of the concern he felt. What effect had the brief episode of gratuitous violence had on her seven-year-old mind?

Jennifer and Richard had moved out of London when they decided to start a family. It was a policy decision. They wanted to raise their children amidst the wholesome influences of nature. Neither of them knew much about nature at that time, but having made a lot of money in the endemic property speculation of the 1980s they could afford to experiment. They settled in a large cottage on an acre and a half a hundred miles to the west of the capital.

What had started as wanting to live outside the strains and stress of city life became, by degrees, an honest attempt to live a life which was ecologically sound.

"It is only an attempt," Richard would say when old friends from London came to stay.

"We just do the best we can," Jennifer said while serving glasses of her delicious elderflower champagne. "The more you find out, the more you realise how difficult it is to really live in harmony with nature."

But they both felt they had gone a long way toward that goal. On their plot of land there were chickens roaming freely, and at least a quarter of the ground was given over to a kitchen garden which supplied vegetables for soup (every day). They took it in turns to bake bread because it was therapeutic. They made yoghurt, chutney, and jam. They bought midlothian pinhead oats in bulk for porridge. Cooking and heating were done with a fuel stove which burnt wood.

"I know it's a fossil fuel," said Richard, "but it is a renewable resource."

The house was thatched. "Marvellous insulation," said Richard.

A section of the garden was left to grow wild in the hope that nature spirits discouraged by the progress of Industrial Man would find haven there. A visiting uncle had once claimed to have seen a fairy in this wild patch, but when Florence was told, she said with utter seriousness, "I don't think you could have seen one."

"Why not?" asked the uncle.

"Because they don't like to be seen."

And the uncle owned as how it might have been a trick of the light.

The ultimate plan was to acquire the field behind the house and fill it with trees. In the meantime, there was a small windmill which could supply electricity in a high wind. There was a water butt and an irrigation system based on a leaky hose. There were several aerobic compost bins, and there were solar panels on the south side of the garage roof. In the garage itself, which was now Richard's studio, was a bicycle for Florence, a tandem, which was really a souvenir from courting days, and a tricycle with a cart attached for shopping in the village. It was a rural idyll. It was a far cry from their former life.

It was the mid-1980s when they moved, and the property boom was in full flood. People would leave their homes in the morning to go to work, knowing that by the time they came back in the evening their flat or house would have made more money that day than they had. It was a very happy and amusing time for millions of people. The only people for whom it wasn't happy or amusing were those who had mismanaged the circumstances of their birth to such an extent that there was no inherited wealth in their family, or, worse still, showed such appalling lack of initiative as to become teachers or nurses. But of course, if these people couldn't afford to play monopoly with their lives they had only themselves to blame, and they were not to be taken seriously in the heady speculative greed of the hour. And while the cost of living space doubled, trebled, and doubled again, wreaking havoc on a generation's hopes of affordable housing, more and more people without homes of any kind appeared on London's streets.

Jennifer was an interior designer, and Richard was an artist. While Jennifer sold her customers ever more trendy design schemes, complete with trompe l'oeil, rag-rolling, and coloured tiling grout, Richard used his painting skills to paint their own flats white and magnolia, achieving an effect which was deeply ordinary and easily saleable. Jennifer had more work than she could handle, and although Richard only occasionally sold a painting, through the succession of flats and then houses which they bought and sold as quickly as the avoidance of capital gains tax allowed, together they made a fortune.

"What do you want?" Richard asked Jennifer one day after work as they sipped Frascati on their patio. There was still paint on his hands from the final coat of gloss to the front door, but the house was already on the market.

"I want a bath with herbs. Then I want you to make passionate love to me. After that, I'll have a plate of pasta, a glass of red wine, and a green salad."

"Yes. I mean in life. What do you want in life?"

"Oh Richard," said Jennifer, "I thought you'd never ask. I want to wake up in the mornings and see green fields and trees. I want to hear birds sing. I still want you to make love to me. I want a child."

"So do I," said Richard. That was nearly eight years ago.

Sitting at breakfast this morning, Richard wondered if they had made the right decision. Perhaps Florence would not be prepared for the brusqueness of modern life, which, after all, she must encounter at some point.

He remembered last week's visit to Marie. Their nearest neighbour was a sculptress who lived a quarter of a mile away. Richard would visit her when he needed advice. She had the gift of reading tea leaves. Sitting in Marie's studio, he told her about the great change in his outlook that had come when his daughter was born.

"Before I was a parent, I was quite prepared for Western Civilisation to slide into the sea. But now, now that there's every chance that it might, I want there to be a world for my girl to grow up in."

"You sound surprised," said Marie. "Isn't that a perfectly natural thing to feel?"

"I suppose it is."

"Well, the world's been going on for a great while now, and perhaps it'll go on for a bit longer."

Richard looked hard at the old Scotswoman's face. Old and wrinkled as it was, with it's bright blue eyes and dancing smile it seemed one of the youngest faces and certainly one of the happiest that he knew. He looked around at the sculptress's studio, and his gaze fell on the pelican she had made. The bird seemed to speak to him. "Go on," it squawked, "Ask her. Trust her. She'll know."

"Marie . . . " he began.

"Now I'll just put the kettle on. You'll stay to tea, and over tea we'll have our talk."

They sat with their tea, and watched by all the animals that Marie had made, Richard told her what was troubling him.

"It's just this life of mine, the way we live I mean, I mean we do all this green stuff, because we believe in it—well we do now, that was another change that came with Florence—and we both thought the country would be better for a child to grow up in, but I wonder sometimes, if it's a bit worthy you know. I wonder if Jennifer's getting a bit bored. She's been gloomy lately. I couldn't bear it if she were unhappy."

"What's made you feel all this?"

"A few weeks ago we were taking a walk, and she suddenly turned to me and said she wished there were a bit more frivolity in our lives. And—it sound's silly—but I was completely dumbfounded. I didn't have a thing to say."

"Have you finished your tea? Good. Now give me your cup."

Marie took his teacup and tilted it one way and another chuckling to herself as she did so. Richard watched her intently and her face seemed to shimmer a little in the afternoon light of her studio. It occurred to him that Marie was the sort of person who made people believe in fairies, but something in her smile and eyes told him he need not say so, she knew it already.

"You're going to go on a little journey—perhaps Florence will go with you? Yes, I think she will. Oh, and you will enjoy yourselves. And then comes something a little puzzling, but never mind that. Oh, and then something very successful. Now Richard, close your eyes and make a wish—don't tell me what it is."

Richard closed his eyes and wished. At the sound of Marie slapping the teacup he opened them, as she exclaimed, "Oh! Yes! You're going to get that, no doubt about it."

"But, Marie, am I making her happy?"

"Och. Let me say something a little sharp to you, as your friend. You have a demon sitting on your shoulder telling you how your life ought to be and how not. And you feel guilty about making all that money, as you feel it's at the expense of others. Accept yourself. Remember Richard, all of us that walk in the sun cast shadows."

Richard gasped at the exact accuracy of what the old sculptress said; she had almost read his thoughts.

"Go home now Richard, and maybe in a day or two take a little journey, but be sure to take Florence with you."

"See," croaked the pelican, "Told you she'd know, told you, told you."

When he got home Jennifer was baking. Loaves, biscuits, cakes. He came up to her and put his arms around her.

"Careful," said Jennifer, "You'll get flour on you."

"Marie sends her love and says thanks for the lettuces."

"That's nice, Richard. I do like her you know."

She pulled away to go on kneading. Richard held her still.

"Jenny, you're not bored are you?"

There was just a small pause, and sharp glance. And then, "What me? No . . . I think Florence might be though. Why don't you take her up to London. She's been dying to go ever since you promised at Christmas."

It was to be a full day trip. There were homemade treacle biscuits and a thermos of tea for the train (they never travelled by car), and packed sandwiches for lunch with a bottle of fizzy orange. Lunch was to be on a rowing boat on the Serpentine and luckily it was a flawless August day with a kind sun and a light breeze, and the highlight was a cream tea at Fortnum & Mason's. In between meals there was a visit to the Planetarium and to Madame Tussaud's, across the park to the museums, and after tea to Hamley's the toyshop. "One more thing we have to do before we go home," said Richard.

Father and daughter walked hand in hand along Oxford Street and when they came to Selfridges they went inside. "You'll help me choose, Florence," said Richard.

They needed to get to the fifth floor, and decided to take the lift up and come down by escalator. The lift filled with people, and they found themselves pressed against the back wall. Directly in front of them stood a buxom lady of perhaps forty years old. She was wearing a musky perfume and lots of eye shadow. Next to her stood a besuited young man of timid aspect. He seemed to be a lot younger than the lady next to him, and the sort of man that defers to the world.

At the second floor more people got in and it became uncomfortably crowded in the lift. Somewhere between the second and third floors the buxom lady turned to the timid young man and, without a word, slapped him in the face. Slapped him quite hard too. The young man turned very red in the face. Not a word was said by anyone, but a silent embarrassment spread like gas and by the time they reached the fifth floor the lift was almost empty.

Richard and Florence found just what they were looking for.

"Should we get them in lemon or pink, Florence?" asked Richard.

"I think lemon for Mummy's colouring."

"And the white lace trim and buttons?"

"Exactly," said Florence.

"We've got a present for you Jenny," said Richard the next morning. "Don't get up. Back in a flash."

"It's from London Mummy," said Florence. And she handed Jennifer a large gift-wrapped package.

"What's this?"

"Open it and see," chirped Florence.

"Silk pyjamas!" Jennifer exclaimed. "Silk pyjamas! What a lovely present. Oh what a beautiful colour. And Richard, Florence, how frivolous."

"I'll go and put the porridge on," said Florence and she ran off.

It was a intimate moment for the parents watching their child's delight. "She loved it in London yesterday. But I'm a bit worried about something." And Richard told her about the incident in the lift.

"I see," Jennifer said. "You must talk to her about it. Was she a nice looking lady?"

"Yes I suppose she was."

"Well start with that then."

"Florence," said Richard, as they sat at breakfast. "Florence, wasn't that a nice looking lady who slapped that man's face in Selfridge's lift yesterday?"

Florence looked up from her cornflakes, and regarded her father steadily. Richard returned her gaze. He hoped that his expression betrayed none of the concern he felt. What effect had the brief episode of gratuitous violence had on her seven-year-old mind.

"I didn't think she was nice at all," said Florence. "She trod on my toe, so I pinched her bottom."

Tone Deaf

Tone Deaf

ON TUESDAY MORNINGS it was singing, and all week. Roger dreaded it. Monday evenings after supper were the worst time because, being a free evening, there was nothing to occupy him until bed. The other boys all seemed to settle happily to something. Some with books, some watching television from 7 P.M. until 8:45 P.M. as was allowed, most would gather around the snooker table and watch the seniors play, a few sat at chess.

Roger used to pace between these groups hoping that no one would notice his distress. He could not go to bed until after cocoa at 9:30 because that would be commented on. Then at least the activity was organised until lights out—boys undressing, taking baths, and, painfully for Roger, singing snatches of songs at each other. Flicking each other with towels, getting the pyjamas on before last bell. But once all was quiet, Roger was always the last to sleep. Flurries of nervous energy running through his body set his mind and heart racing.

When Tuesday morning came, he tried to tell himself that it was Wednesday, the awful singing class was over and it wouldn't come again for a whole week. For seven whole days he would not endure that burning shame when he couldn't hit the notes. He wouldn't be longing for the class to be over so that he could sprint down to the kitchen garden in the first break and burst into tears behind the beach tree where he wouldn't be seen. And in a whole week, anything could happen. Mr. Hunstanton might die.

At ten o'clock, the boys filed into the music room and remained standing until the girls from the school across the village had sat down. It was the one occasion during the week when the two junior groups were put together. Roger wished it could have been any other activity. The seniors had dancing; even that, which was alarming to say the least, would have been preferable to this.

The girls came in, there were glances and giggles. The girls sat, the boys sat, more looking and laughing. Mr. Hunstanton came to the door, instantly the room fell quiet. He entered, and the class stood up.

"Be seated," growled the old musician.

It was known that Mr. Hunstanton was over sixty-five, because he could have retired but had chosen not to. No one knew how much older than sixty-five he was. To Roger he seemed a hundred and fifty, and because he had taken fright at his first sight of the old man, and because singing was a closed book to him, it was like being in the same room with an ogre.

The truth was that Mr. Hunstanton was a poor musician who wished he were a better one. His clumsiness at the piano—an instrument which he loved—made him impatient, and his long life of underachievement had left him bitter. To his credit, he meant no harm.

"Solos today," said Mr. Hunstanton. "Five good marks for the first volunteer."

There was giggling.

"Quiet!"

Mr. Hunstanton's eye fell upon Malcolm. Malcolm was the music master's favourite, everyone's favourite. One of those people to whom success in everything seemed to come effortlessly, he also excelled at singing. Malcolm stood up.

"I'll sing, sir."

Mr. Hunstanton smiled a rare smile. "Good boy," he said.

Roger was terrified that he might be picked. He stole a glance at the clock. Four minutes had passed since the start of the lesson; Malcolm's solo might last two or three minutes more. Mr. Hunstanton would spend another minute at least after that praising Malcolm and pointing out how easy it was. So that was eight minutes. Which left thirty-seven unaccounted for. There were twenty-four of them in the class. So, number of people in the class, minus one which was Malcolm, over time taken to sing, that figure into thirty-seven, meant that his chances of being safely ignored were at best one in two, or at worst—oh no—about one in five. Roger felt the tingling sensation of fear in his stomach. "Please don't let him pick me. Please don't," he began saying to himself over and over.

Malcolm was singing now. There was no question about it, he sang beautifully. The room was unusually quiet, even the roudiest listening to Malcolm's voice as it gave the perfect centre of each note. Roger wished he could sing like that. As he listened to the pure sound, he felt as if he were uniting with it, as if it were coming out of him too. He shook himself to his senses, some part of him knew that this sense of unity with Malcolm's singing was a dangerous illusion. He looked around the room and noticed how everyone exuded approval. Wouldn't it be great to be on the receiving end of that?

A new thought came to Roger. Why shouldn't he sing too? He had never attempted a solo before. His terrible discomfort came simply from feeling at odds with the sounds around him. And Mr. Hunstanton had never given him any direct instruction. Forgotten for a moment were all the sensations of fear that the mere mention of singing classes had triggered in him. Surely he should try. No, no. It would be too awful to have to stand up in front of everyone—some of them were bound to laugh. But even so, why shouldn't he try? The worst that could happen would be that he wouldn't do it very well, and even if they did laugh at him, so what?

Now Mr. Hunstanton was talking. "You see, it's not so difficult. Now, who's going to be next?"

Roger stood up immediately, not giving himself time for a second thought. "Please sir," he heard himself say. Mr. Hunstanton looked so surprised that Roger couldn't say anything else. He didn't understand why Mr. Hunstanton looked surprised at all. After all, he had been in the music class for months now, and Mr. Hunstanton took them for scripture as well. True, the old man had never spoken directly to him, but surely he knew who he was. Why was he surprised? "So you'd like to have a go, would you?"

Roger's courage was wavering now. Why had he risked it? He should have stayed quiet. Chances were he wouldn't have been picked. But now it was too late, he was on his feet. He could feel all eyes in the room turned on him. From somewhere behind he heard a chuckle, he reddened and nodded.

"Page twenty. First verse only, once through."

Roger opened the song book. Mr. Hunstanton went to the piano and bashed out an introduction and nodded at Roger to come in. Roger willed sound to come out of him, but none did. "Take a breath, boy!" yelled Mr. Hunstanton above the bashing of the piano keys, and started the introduction again.

Roger took a breath, which made him feel sick, and launched into the first line. From the start, he knew it wasn't going to go well. He could hear his voice faltering, nowhere near the notes. Just keep going he told himself. Just finish it. But now he couldn't see the words very clearly. He started to snatch quick short breaths, and then he turned bright red, because—terror—he thought he might cry. He musn't do that whatever happened. His words became mumbles, and rather than let the tears out, which he knew must happen if he carried on trying to sing, he just stopped.

Mr. Hunstanton stopped playing the piano and looked at Roger. There was a silence. "Well," began Mr. Hunstanton not unkindly, "it's very sad, and quite unusual, but you are what we call tone deaf."

Roger nodded.

"So I don't want you to sing in these classes. You can mouth the words if you want to, but don't make a noise. Understand?"

Roger stood still, staring at the old man. Unable even to nod.

Another chuckle from behind.

"Quiet!" roared Mr. Hunstanton. He turned to Roger, "Go and sit down now."

Somehow Roger got to his seat, and somehow the minutes passed. At least it was all over. He was numb with shame, but he was safe now; he need never sing again.

For a whole year Roger never did open his mouth to sing. Not once. In the singing classes he dutifully mouthed the words, and he did the same when the school went to church on Sundays, and he never made a sound. He wasn't terrified of singing now, because it was so simple—he just couldn't sing.

So why was it then that almost a year to the day later Roger tried again? He couldn't think why. Some vestige of hope in him wanted another chance. He wasn't sure if Mr. Hunstanton knew his name, or knew who he was. The old man never spoke to him or acknowledged his presence in any way, so he stood up for a solo expecting to be allowed to try again. Mr. Hunstanton turned on him and said with deep conviction, "I've told you. You're tone deaf. Sit down."

Roger sat, there was no pain or embarrassment. It was an easy mistake to make. He thought he might try to sing again, but of course, silly of him to forget, he was tone deaf. He would never try again.

Six months later Mr. Hunstanton died. When he was officially mourned, Roger was conscious of no feeling at all for this man whom he had once hated and feared; he was merely indifferent.

The new music master was Mr. Hall, a young man who had grown a beard so as to look older and more authoritative. Waiting for Mr. Hall for the first time, it dawned on Roger that he might be required to make a sound. No, surely not, he was tone deaf.

Mr. Hall came in. The class shuffled to its feet. "Yes, yes, yes. Don't bother with all that. Sit down, sit down." He looked at them and smiled. "Christmas is coming up, so we'll do some carols I think. Yes, that's it, we'll all blast away together today, and then later on, over the next few weeks, I'm going to do some individual work with each of you. Get to know your voices. All right, 'Once in Royal David's . . .' good and loud everybody, see if we can take the roof off."

There was interest in the room. This sounded like a radical approach. The class blasted away as encouraged, all except Roger who just mouthed the words. Twice Mr. Hall caught his eye, but he was smiling. Roger felt as if he were trying to be invisible as well as inaudible, and he thought he was successful, but as the class was leaving, Mr. Hall beckoned Roger to him.

"Roger isn't it?"

"Yes sir."

Mr. Hall extended his hand. "Bernard Hall. Pleased to meet you."

They shook hands.

"Tell me Roger, do you like singing? Point is, I noticed that you weren't. Why was that then?"

"Mr. Hunstanton told me not to sir."

"What?"

"Mr. Hunstanton said I was tone deaf sir."

"He did what?"

Roger looked at Mr. Hall, who seemed to be very angry about something. Then suddenly he smiled gently at Roger and said "It's all right, Roger. Look, could you tell me exactly how this happened? Tell me the whole thing. Could you do that?"

For no reason that he understood, Roger couldn't find words to say anything. Mr. Hall put a hand on the boy's shoulder.

"I tried to sing a solo sir, and . . . I . . . I couldn't do it very well . . . I tried but . . ."

Tears were in the boy's eyes now and he was red like a beetroot.

"And what happened then?"

The sound of Mr. Hall's voice, friendly, concerned, and caring, was too much for Roger; the last of his self-control dissolved. He cried as he could have cried but hadn't the morning of that terrible lesson. He would have broken away and run off, but his new teacher held him gently and firmly by the shoulders. After a while Roger looked up, and Mr. Hall smiled friendship at him. "Tell me the rest, Roger," he said.

Roger told it all very matter of factly now the tears were gone. How he had been told he was tone deaf and not to sing. How he had tried again and been told not to try.

"Do you know what tone deaf means?" asked Mr. Hall.

"Someone who can't tell one note from another sir."

"That's right. And is that you?"

"I don't know sir."

Mr. Hall went to the piano, he stabbed at middle C.

"Sing ahh for me on that note."

Roger sang ahh a full tone flat.

"Yes, that's very good," said Mr. Hall quietly. "Try this one." He pressed another key, the ahh was still flat—but less so than the first time.

"Well you're certainly not tone deaf," said Mr. Hall. He came and stood opposite Roger again. "Roger, I have something very important to say to you, and when I've said it, I want you to repeat it back to me. Can you do that?"

"Yes sir."

"Good man. Now, look me straight in the eye, and listen carefully. Are you ready?"

"Yes sir."

"Good." Mr. Hall's eyes were now fixed on Roger's and Roger felt that Mr. Hall was about to communicate something fundamental to him.

"Mr. Hunstanton," said Bernard Hall slowly, "was a silly old sod."

For a moment there was only the sound of Roger's jaw hitting the floor. He burst into squeals of laughter and Mr. Hall laughed too. "It will be better now, Roger," he said.

In time it was better. Roger was never to be a singer that others would pay to come and hear, but all his life it gave him great pleasure to sing in his bath.

Capital Gains
A Thirty-Minute Radio Play

Capital Gains
A Thirty-Minute Radio Play

CHARACTERS

Julius Hutch, a retired debtor with a philosophical cast of
   mind.
Pauline Tone, loans advisor at the bank, more compassion-
   ate than strictly necessary.

OTHER CORRESPONDENTS

F. H. Warming
A. Twhark
Holly Barker
E. H. Matrix
Stanley Hart
R. Goole
G. Whistle
H. Pibble

Loans Office,
The High Street Bank plc,
101 High Street,
London North West.

Dear Mr. Hutch,

As of the close of business today, your current account stands at £1427.63 overdrawn. Please contact us immediately upon receipt of this letter, and make arrangements to put the account into credit at your earliest convenience.

Yours sincerely,

Mrs. P. Tone
Lending Advisor

P. S. Mr. Hutch, I shouldn't really write any more, but I did enjoy our chat the other day, you really made me laugh. In view of your general financial situation, what with the repossession of your home and so forth, this computer letter seems to add insult to injury. Just to say, I know what it's like to run out of money too, and send sympathy.

Credit Management Control & Sanctions,
Harvestcard,
Milton Mobray,
Herts H30 9PU.

Dear Mr. Hutch,

Thank you for your payment of £100 last month. Unfortunately, this was insufficient to meet the minimum payment required. The balance on your credit card is currently £2,213.12. This is £213.12 in excess of your credit limit. Please send a remittance of £213.12 immediately, and the remainder of the minimum payment by the fourth of next month.

Yours sincerely,

F. H. Warming
Credit Supervisor

BRITISH TELECOME,
(PENSIONERS' ACCESS DIVISION),
BT TOWERS,
MIDDLE VALE,
LEICESTER LE17 H5.

Dear Mr. Hutch,

We recently sent you a final demand for payment of your telephone account. As yet no payment has been received. We regret to inform you that your telephone has been disconnected. If you have sent a payment within the last seven days, please ignore this letter. There will be a charge for reconnection.

Yours sincerely,

A. Twhark
Regional Manager

BARGAINSAVE,
ONE, ON THE MALL,
TEDDYBOROUGH SUPER MARE,
WEST KENT UP11 OY.

Dear Mr Hutch,

Congratulations!

You may already have won £50,000.

Simply return your winning numbers in the special YES! envelope. Don't forget to include your completed game card as well, which will give you one of three fantastic free gifts when you place your first order with us.

Or you may prefer a generous 20% discount on your entire first year's shopping.

And remember! If you reply within seven days, we will double—yes double!—the first prize to a fantastic £100,000. All you have to do is simply post your entry in the prepaid YES! envelope, we will then send you your personalised home shopping catalogue.

Just think, Mr. Hutch, of what you could do with £100,000! A new car? The conservatory extension you've always wanted? Perhaps a new luxury kitchen? And plenty left over for a fabulous holiday for two in the sun.

No purchase is necessary to enter the prize draw, but home shopping with Bargainsave opens the door to a fantastic range of amazing items at unbeatable prices. So don't miss out. Post the YES! envelope today!

Best wishes for your success,

Holly Barker
Customer Servicer

National Power Barter,
Code: LASTRESORT,
Electric Lane,
Biddlefasting BO1 GUM.

Dear Mr. Hutch,

It has been necessary to disconnect your electricity supply due to nonpayment of accounts. There will be a charge for reconnecting the supply. If you have sent a payment within the last seven days, please ignore this letter.

Yours faithfully,

E. H. Matrix
Area Controller

**Value Book Club,
The Uppers,
Belgrave Estate Park,
Bletchington,
Hants HO14.**

Dear Mr. Hutch,

We are surprised to see that you have not settled last month's payment of £3.76. Surely you do not wish to tarnish your record as a respected customer with Value Book Club. If the amount is not paid in full, we shall be forced to take further action to recover it.

Sincerely,

G. Whistle
Reader's Friend

PEOPLE'S GAS GB,
DEPT SAD,
SUITE 11, THE PIPES,
GRAVETOWN,
SURREY FA3.

Dear Mr. Hutch,

After various attempts to contact you, we have reluctantly taken the decision to discontinue the supply of gas to your home. In line with our new guidelines of care as specified in our customers charter, if you feel you qualify for our special-needs category, please do not hesitate to contact our helpline which is open between the hours of 3:20 P.M. and 4:45 P.M. on alternate Tuesdays. If payment has been made within the last seven days, we apologise for troubling you with this advice. In such a case your supply will be reconected at a reduced charge once your payment has been cleared.

Yours sincerely,

Stanley Hart
Customer Relations Officer

THE TOWN HALL,
HAMBLE WARD OFFICE,
GRAND GAP,
HENDLE,
NORTH WEST LONDON.

Mr. J. Hutch,

Nonpayment of community charge.
Notice of Intended Distress.

All remittances must now be payable to the Bailiff at the address given and not the council. Any money paid to the council does not invalidate the cost due under this order.

Amount for which this Distress is made (including Arrears to Authority, Court Costs, Levy Fee plus VAT): £452.73

And take further notice that unless the said amounts be paid inclusive of all costs and charges within seven days the bailiff will make further attendance to levy distress.

Signed: *H. Pibble*

Authorised

Customer Enticement,
Maxiflexiplan House,
Little Barston,
Cumbria, CU1.

Dear Mr Hutch,

Having trouble coping with life's expenses?

Don't worry. The answer is just a phone call away. With today's low interest rates, there's never been a better time to borrow money. Apply today for an Easi-Loan.

The table below shows how you can settle all your other bills at a stroke. And if you take out our special Maxiflexi scheme for large borrowers you get even better rates.

Simply fill in the application form giving full details of your monthly income and expenses. We at Easi-Loan will do the rest.

Your home is at risk if you do not keep up payments . . .

Looking forward to serving you,

R. Goole
Enticement Officer

The Larches,
Nightingale Crescent,
London North West.

From Julius Hutch

To All My Creditors

Dear Sirs,

I am not a wealthy man.

To open this correspondence with such a bland and bald statement may seem to you unnecessary, as I am sure, in this age of credit reference, you are already aware of the fact.

But to me . . .

Ah, to me, the open utterance of that testimony is in fact significant if only in the psychological sense. (In material senses, I have known it all my life.) But it appears to me now, now that your name is legion, that the admittance of my poverty is a significant confronting of the shadow which has dogged me all my life.

In this modern age when conveniences of every sort are available to all types and makes of man, I find myself in reduced circumstances on the brink of financial ruin.

To you and your computerised correspondence, what significance can attach to the falling off of one of your accounts? But to me, the solemn experiencer of this fate, a more organic response is called for.

I count my life a failure. Since early manhood, I have struggled to put bread upon the table for myself, my wife (now dead), and my children (now grown and flown) with always only partial success. The state of my indebtedness has at all times been greater than I would have wished, and at no time less. Now, responsible for myself alone, at the fag end of my life on Earth, I find pecuniary pressure at last bursting through the damn of my labours and the tide of insolvency about to sweep in flood through all the efforts of my life. My assets are not large, not sufficient, I fear, to satisfy all monetary claims upon me.

At such a pass, what refuge of comfort might a man find? I take solace from the writings of Marcus Aurelius, who, although a Roman Emperor and one assumes never short of a crust, advised that the only wisdom in life is to accept it all. Therefore, I am resolved to watch the ensuing drama of possession, repossession, and seizure as a spectator at a play. I shall observe your actions, the inevitable consequence of my inability to pay, as one indifferent.

I bear none of you ill will, and I address you all the several signatories of these several final demands, in the spirit of our common humanity, wishing you nothing but well.

When in due process of legality you have taken all I possess, it is my fervent hope that I may endure to wish you still well. And, naked of wealth, return to my creator acknowledging a life lived committing every kind of mistake, but most especially mistakes of a financial flavour.

I have the honour Sirs to remain your most humble and obedient servant.

Yours sincerely,

Julius Hutch

P. S. Mrs. Tone, how kind of you to add a few words of your own to the computer letter. You are the human face of credit, and I thank you!

LOANS OFFICE,
THE HIGH STREET BANK PLC,
101 HIGH STREET,
LONDON NORTH WEST.

Dear Mr. Hutch,

Thank you for your letter which arrived here two days ago. We do not usually advise customers of credits to their accounts, but in view of the contents of your letter, I thought it appropriate to inform you that we have today credited by telegraphic transfer £4,601,740.72 to your account from the Bank of Hong Kong & the Islands.

Should you require further details on this matter please do not hesitate to contact us.

Yours sincerely,

Mrs. P. Tone
Lending Advisor

The Larches,
Nightingale Crescent,
London North West.

My Dear Mrs. Tone,

How shall I put this?

I was surprised to say the least, by your last letter, and admit to having thought I was the victim of a cruel and tasteless practical joke. A swift visit to the cash dispenser, where I checked my balance, has proved this not to be the case.

Would you be kind enough to confirm the following in writing?

1. The credit of £4,601,740.72 has indeed been correctly placed at my account.

2. These funds are available for use immediately.

Awaiting your reply by return.

Sincerely yours,

Kind regards,

Julius Hutch

LOANS OFFICE,
THE HIGH STREET BANK PLC,
101 HIGH STREET,
LONDON NORTH WEST.

Dear Mr. Hutch,

As per your request, I can confirm the following points.
1. The money has been placed in your account in accordance with instructions received from the Bank of Hong Kong & the Islands.
2. The money is indeed available for immediate use.
Of course, you are aware of the position on this last point, as I notice that you have this morning withdrawn all but £1 from your current account. The remaining pound will be sufficient to keep your account with us open.
If you require any further information, please do not hesitate to contact me. Customers in receipt of an unusually large sum often consult with our financial advisor. I would be happy to make an appointment for you.

Yours sincerely,

Mrs. P. Tone
Lending Advisor

INTERNATIONAL TRANSFERS,
THE BANK OF HONG KONG & THE ISLANDS,
HONG KONG.
TELEX DIVISION

Dear Sirs,

It has come to our notice that in the previous month's trading a substantial amount was wrongly sent to your bank for credit to one of your accounts. The amount in question was some 4½ million pounds sterling. The credit was due to a clerical error. We should be greatly obliged if you would institute a search for any such credits deposited in accounts where such credits were not expected.

Thanking you in anticipation,

Yours faithfully,

Peter Fang
Senior Divisional Executive

As of,
The Larches,
Nightingale Crescent,
London North West.

My Dear Mrs. Tone,

I should have written sooner! I hope you will accept my apologies, and believe me when I say that recent weeks have been rather busy. But I am getting ahead of myself.

After your kind and prompt verification of the deposit to my account, I found myself in a state of some agitation. To be perfectly truthful with you (now that it is safe to do so), I never expected to have a large sum of money at any time in my life at all, and certainly not now that my strength and earning capacity is failing.

Agitated as I was, I made a pot of camomile tea, my usual beverage when nervously overstimulated, but even after three cups, I found the agitation persisted. Senses of shock, excitement, inexplicably fearfulness. Upon reflection, I found what perturbed me most was the daunting weight of responsibility at how to use creatively this financial gain given to me by the will of fate.

Various options flashed through my mind. I could attempt to return the money, but I believe I have already mentioned (somewhere, obliquely perhaps) that it may have been mistakenly deposited, and I understand after taking legal advice that within the strict letter of the law that is all I am required to do. So that deals with that option. I am resolved not to think of it further.

Strange that extreme financial good fortune should present its own trauma. One has heard of people who win millions on the pools and continue in humdrum jobs, in effect stashing their winnings under the psychological floorboards and never looking at them. Denying, in fact, that the power of change has entered their lives.

The first requirement of my creative action in this matter is that I should be a fit and able instrument of use. Therefore, I have prescribed myself a three-month holiday. I am resolved to travel in conditions of the greatest possible comfort and surround myself with luxuries. I envisage fine wines, delicate viands, and leisurely sexual recreation with partners of great beauty. This last possibility I venture forth in playful spirit. As you may know, I am now an elderly gentleman, and it had been some time since I indulged in the universal pastime. Nonetheless, if the chance comes my way, I shall not refuse it—that would be churlish!

Well now, to the practical arrangements. As you know, wealth creates wealth. This extraordinary fact, borne in upon me with new force, seems already a simple principle. I have divided my windfall in two after paying off my what now seem insignificant debts—perspective changes everything doesn't it? Without hundreds of thousands to one's name, the want of a figure as paltry as ten or fifteen thousand pounds is enough to ruin a life, make misery; whereas in the opposite position the same sum seems no more than a little overspending during a morning at the shops! After resolving my debts, I have apportioned £250,000 for present use. The rest is safely, anonymously, placed in high-interest Swiss bank accounts where the collective interest will amount to nearly £10,000 pounds a week—another charming effect of capitalism when experienced from above.

Of course, these arrangements took a little time to prepare, truth to tell, and that is why you have not heard from me sooner. But financially inexperienced as I was, I was delighted to find that what I had believed all my life—namely, that if suddenly endowed I would know exactly what to do with it—was true. Cash opened many doors for me, and my schemes for untraceable adventure are now in place. It goes without saying, of course, that by the time you read this I shall be gone.

My mind is plunging, raging, thronging with schemes for use of the money. But for the moment I intend to devote myself entirely to the pursuit of restorative pleasure.

I look upon you now, Mrs. P. Tone, as a valued friend, a colleague almost. Please find enclosed two tickets for *Phantom of the Opera*, a half-pound box of Swiss Truffles (I do hope they have survived the post), and a book token for £50. On this last, if you are looking for food for thought you could do worse than peruse the *Dialogues of Plato*—I can recommend the Jowett translation.

And on that note, my dear Mrs. P. Tone, at the moment of my departure for foreign climes, I wish you only well.

Kind regards,

Cordially yours,

Julius Hutch

Loans Office,
The High Street Bank plc,
101 High Street,
London North West.

Dear Mr. Hutch,

Thank you for your last letter and enclosures.

The Bank of Hong Kong & the Islands has contacted us in respect of the £4,601,740.72 credited to your account back in January. I enclose a copy of their correspondence with us.

This is a matter you may wish to take up with them directly. Technically we have no further responsibility in the matter, having acted in accordance with their initial instructions and responded to your own letters.

As a matter of interest, we did follow the usual checking procedures stipulated for very large amounts, but the Bank of Hong Kong & the Islands insisted that everything was in order.

Thank you for the gifts. Very kind and generous of you I am sure. Unfortunately, it was not felt appropriate by my boss that I make use of them. But thank you all the same.

Cordially yours,

Mrs. P. Tone

As of,
The Larches,
Nightingale Crescent,
London North West.

Dear Mrs. Tone,

What you must think of me! Nine months almost to the day since your last and no answer yet!

This is due in part to the possibly overcomplicated forwarding arrangements I made on leaving Britain, arrangements which I shan't bore you with here. And also it must be admitted that during these last months I have presented something of a moving target.

Allow me to bring you up to date. It has been a real odyssey. I did not stay long in Paris. No more than twenty-four hours; I wanted to move on. The sudden surge of power through my financial veins gave me at first boundless energy, and extreme good health. I was more active and alert than in many years.

I was strolling through the Paris boulevards contemplating the hiring of a car when I suddenly realised that a little extravagance might be in order. Accordingly, I bought a two-seater Lagonda fifty in forest green. I bought it for cash.

Paris to St. Tropez took three days. I made brief stops in Beaune and Aix-en-Provence, acquainting myself with those fine wines of which I had dreamt. When I saw the Azure Coast, I allowed myself to slow down, for at last I felt myself properly abroad. I booked a suite at the Metropole, and the luxury was magnificent—so was the price—and it pricks any stoic strain in my character to admit how thrilling it was to watch high denomination banknotes flow from my pockets, and to know that for present purposes the supply was infinite.

I gave myself seven days, and incidentally nights, for the life of the senses. It was an unfettered indulgence in the balm of spring. Leisurely chauffeuring by day along the precipitate roads, no less leisurely recreation in the universal pastime by night—at my age one does not rush. And here I may say that I was delighted to find that I was still sufficiently youthful to indulge.

At the end of that Bacchanal week, I scanned the port until I found what I was looking for. A young couple gazing deep into each other's eyes, an aura of romance upon them. I would like to say that they reminded me of my own courting days; alas not so, my own marriage was contracted in nothing like so romantic a setting. I approached them, and over a liqueur explained that the sports car standing on the boulevard was now theirs if they would care to accept it.

I had a list of places to visit, places I had wanted to see all my life. The Pyramids. Ayers Rock. The Temple at Delphi. The Preservation Hall in New Orleans. I was in a hurry; frankly, at my time of life, one doesn't know when the egg timer will go ping!

Followed then the main part of my travels. I moved around a good deal, visiting sites of natural beauty or archaeological interest. I saw exotic cities and tasted the best in each that money could buy. In all, I circled the globe and visited all continents. And the distilled impression of this of necessity hasty travel is that, on all the Earth, among all peoples, the same hopes, concerns, and fears visit us all. The chap who wrote Ecclesiastes was right: "There is nothing new under the sun."

At length, wearied rather by constant movement, a new need made itself felt. I wanted now a secluded place for reflection, and to digest the surfeit of new impressions my mind and senses had received in these past months.

I knew exactly what I was looking for, and am now living in a very remote place—you will forgive me for not describing it in detail. I will merely say that it is as near to paradise on Earth as any of us might expect to get. Picture to yourself your own ideal. What would it be, Mrs. Tone? A lakeside villa in the High Alps? A remote cabin in the maple forests of Canada, where the autumn colours would ravish your eye? Possibly some custom-designed home in the south seas, open to refreshing breezes in the dry season, yet safe against the thrilling drama of the monsoon?

Perhaps paradise is a state of mind. I find now, now so potently delivered from the numbing anxiety that comes with constant (unsuccessful) struggle for money, I find now that it is as if my very consciousness were transformed by the soothing effects of leisure, ease, tranquillity. Let me tell you that our hurt world is still beautiful, but if there is pain in paradise, it is the pain of knowing that so much human life is lived diminished. My belief is (in common with the ancients) that the spark of the universe lives within us all.

But how much greatness is lost to humanity simply crushed by circumstance? Was it for wretched toil in mean purposes that we were made?

I have never been interested in politics. I've had quite enough trouble ordering my own life without wanting to order anyone else's, but something in me yearns to proclaim, "There must be a better way!" Do we not deserve better than to briefly struggle and die? Are we not after all, all of us, children of the stars?

Well . . .

To return to Earth.

I know that certain agents of the Bank of Hong Kong & the Islands are keen to contact me, and I imagine they will attempt to trace me by all available means. As a matter of fact, it was by chance that I first became aware of their desire to talk to me. I was taking a simple supper in a taverna on the south side of Crete, where I chanced upon an old copy of the *Sun* newspaper. I was intrigued but not altogether surprised to see a photograph of myself standing outside my home at Nightingale Close with the headline "Grandpa Bests Bank." The details of the following article were almost accurate and hardly sensationalised at all, but then I suppose it is a fairly sensational story anyway. On this note, thank you for forwarding the relevant correspondence. It does make entertaining reading. The whole catalogue of dismay and fervour reminds me of my favourite maxim, "Hell hath no fury like a vested interest masquerading as a moral principle." Well, all this is a lengthy preamble to my apology for not getting back to you sooner. I hope it goes some way toward explaining.

Now, I must take issue with your refusal to accept my previous small tokens. Surely you appreciate that to a man in my singular position it is a new pleasure to be able to give. In my past life I have wished to be more generous, and one of the unexpected joys of being in receipt of such a hugely enormous sum of money is the thrill of virtuous excitement I have felt at every time I gave some of it away.

Please find enclosed a money order for £10,000 in your favour. On the moral position of entitlement to the money, I have reasoned to myself thus: The philosophies of all peoples tell us that all life is one. Ultimately unity not division. Everything that lives is held in mighty interdependency, and the symbiotic relationships of Sun and Planet, of Culture and Individual, of Banking and Commerce—these forces which drive our lives have but one source. Ultimately, WHOSE MONEY IS IT???

If gift comes into your life, neglect not to receive it for good or ill, and make best use of the adventure that falls to your hand.

Should you wish to continue this correspondence, there is a good chance that I will receive your letters and reply to them, though in the circumstances, I cannot be absolutely certain!

Kind regards,

Cordially yours,

Julius Hutch

Hill Cottage,
Uplands Walk,
Merrygate,
London North West.

Dear Mr. Hutch,

I am writing to you privately and not in my capacity as lending advisor. Thank you for yours which arrived yesterday.

£10,000 is more money than I have ever had before all at once. I have put it in an offshore account where it will earn good interest until this affair is settled one way or another.

In these past few months we've had people from the Bank of Hong Kong & the Islands, and also the police and people from Interpol as well, in our office going over our books and all through our procedures. At first they were all trying to trace the money and convinced they would get it back, but now that so much time has gone by I have to say that here at the bank we are all rather impressed by the way you and the money seem to have completely disappeared.

Thank you so much for the money order.

My warm good wishes to you,

Pauline Tone (Mrs.)

As of,
The Larches,
Nightingale Crescent,
London North West.

Dear Pauline,

I feel we are such old friends now—please call me Julius.

As to my traceability, it's really quite simple. My letters are sent to the PO box number to which you have forwarded them, where they are collected and then sent by a series of homing pigeons to a gentleman of my acquaintance. From there, they are converted into radio signals and transmitted on certain frequencies on the first of each month. My receiver works only one way, as a receiver, and is therefore not traceable. I am sure you know all this, as I am sure that agents of the bank have discovered my system—indeed, their letters indicate as much. But clearly they have decided it is better to be able to communicate with me one way than not at all.

I do not know what I should say were I to meet anyone with a direct interest in the original £4,601,740.72. For, in fact, the greater part of that fortune has passed out of my hands. In my previous letters I have described a part of my adventures and travels. But now that the thirsts of the flesh are quenched (it didn't take long) a larger desire has made itself felt. I want now to live out my remaining days in quietness, and prepare for death, which is after all the greatest adventure, as a philosopher would.

And here comes a problem, for this particular philosopher's life account seems tainted by a final act of criminality. By that I mean use of money which was not "strictly speaking" mine to use. I wonder how many banks could stand so accused? I know nothing of the techniques for growing and harvesting cash. But I wonder if the creation of wealth is arranged quite fairly? If a bank loans millions for the exploitation of some natural resource, and huge profit accrues to multinational corporations on the backs of cheap labour, and further, if that cheap labour is abandoned without means to livelihood when the natural resource is used up, or the whim of the currency exchanges means profit can be found more easily elsewhere, is there theft in such a situation?

Notwithstanding these thoughts on big banking, it continues to prick my conscience that the money cannot in any light be looked on as rightfully mine. However, so deep is my sense of outrage at the way the rich get richer while the poor get poorer that I ultimately resolved to compromise with experiments in the nature of a modern-day Robin Hood. In short, I have given it all away. Well, almost all; I live now a frugal existence, quietly. I have made arrangements so that my needs are supplied for the foreseeable future and it has not been expensive. I find more nourishment in the unspoilt nature where I live now than in any extravagance. I have shelter, clothing, and warmth. A few groceries are all I require to keep body and soul together.

Parting with all this money has been fine sport! I decided to benefact only individuals in need, people crippled by debt, whose lives stood in danger of complete material ruin. Sadly, it has not been hard to find such people, there are so many.

Is it true to say that poverty makes us ugly? That need breeds crime? I think not. I have been shamed time and again witnessing courage in adversity. Courage so much greater than my own in similar circumstances.

I decided that I would pursue benefaction with the same rigour usually given to debt collection. Accordingly, I found access to data held by lending agencies; with the right expertise, it's not difficult. I then had several fictional company letterheads printed. Armed with quantities of bogus stationery and a word processor, I gaily posted cheques for thousands.

Dear Mr. and Mrs. So and so,

Congratulations! The Society of Anonymous Philan-thropists has selected you for its special celebratory award. Enclosed is a cheque in your favour. There are no strings or catches. This money comes to you as a result of your being alive. We urge you to enjoy it.

Or I might say,

Dear Mr. Such and such,

and this one might be headed

"Getting & Spending Ltd."
It has come to our notice that almost all your domes-tic bills are unpaid. This letter exhorts you to use the enclosed banker's draft to stick two fingers up at all your creditors.

At first I dallied with trivial amounts of a few thousands, and than waited to see if the money was accepted. Invari-ably it was. But soon I grew bolder and began to hand over larger amounts, £20,000 here, £50,000 there. Occasionally I would simply do exactly what the Bank of Hong Kong & the Islands did to me; that is, place a large amount unex-plained in a stranger's account and leave them to ponder. That is what the bank did to me, but there was one impor-tant difference; namely, I always made it clear that the money was legitimately due to whomever it was addressed.

To the Bank of Hong Kong & the Islands I decided to make token reparation. Accordingly, I sent them a money order for £46.01. £46.01 is of course an exact fraction of 1 percent of the original, albeit a small fraction. It is in fact, one thousandth of 1 percent, and at £46.01 per month it would take 8,333 years to repay the principal—by which time the compound interest would be unthinkable! But I think it shows willing, and I hope it goes some way toward compensating them for the (not inconsiderable) expense they have incurred in this whole episode. The monthly arrangement of £46.01 will cease at my death.

I have enjoyed our correspondence, and may I say how nicely you have played the interface between the mighty turnings of international banking and one elderly maverick. And so, my dear Pauline, until the next time, have a good time. If there is no next time, have a good life!

Yours with great pleasure,

Julius Hutch

P. S. So pleased that you saw sense over the money order. Forgive the presumption, but I have organised that all your credit cards, store cards, your domestic bills this quarter, the outstanding payments on your car, and your mortgage are all paid off.

Best,

Julius

Small Change

Small Change

SOMETHING BIG has happened to Hubert. I went round yesterday morning for the monthly loathsome shepherd's pie, and it would appear that he's completely changed his life. It's very worrying. The odd thing is, on the way up Pembridge Road I was just wondering if there's any value in keeping up this performance. Boring old fart that Hubert has become. And now this! He might have warned me. After all, I have known him one way and another for thirty weary years. I suppose there is a tired enjoyment in toiling round to his pongy old flat and sniping at him—it is easy to do.

I knew something was up even as I turned the key in the latch. I smelled—of all things—paint! The hallway which used to be lined with secondhand books was completely clear and newly painted all white. Then some strange man came bounding out of the living room muttering something about changing the locks. I actually could not utter.

He didn't look like Hubert. He was wearing cream-coloured chinos, a blue silk shirt, and suede shoes—all ironed and neat. This, mind you, from a man whose usual is cords, some old T-shirt, a sleeveless pullover, and socks with open-toed sandals. And the face! Cancel the scraggy beard, take out the saw-edged parting; in fact, cut and style the whole mop and leave it trim above the ears. Throw away the horn-rimmed specs, and replace with tinted—yes tinted!—lenses. So, as I said, something big.

I certainly wasn't going to ask him any questions. I did my best to go through the motions. I tried to tell him a story about my loathsome neighbours but I couldn't quite get my mind on it. How do you adjust if someone you've known more than half your life suddenly goes adventuring with their identity? But I was determined not to mention it. Wouldn't give him the satisfaction. When I was leaving though, I had to say something.

"Well, you've obviously been enjoying yourself. See you next time then Hubert?"

"If you like," said Hubert. "I'm changing the locks." He said it as if he'd told me before.

"You might have said."

Hubert took a deep breath. He went on, "You might have asked. Anyhow, I am saying, now."

This was entirely new behaviour. "Why?" I managed.

"To do with all the changes, Alice. I've found something useful to do at last."

Well, I left him to it and scuttled away. It's been a symbiotic affair, Platonic. Well, apart from that one night. I couldn't fancy popping back to mine just then. Not after all that, so I decided on a bit of a wander up and down the Portobello Road. Not a brilliant choice in terms of mood improvement—it's the Portobello Road that Hubert and I have always planned on retiring to, to run our antique shop once we've become old and hideous. I popped into a place about halfway down the hill where there's a girl called Caroline who seems to have been selected specially for her rudeness—just my type, she's nice to look at too, always wearing something sprayed on. It quite brightens the day to go and have a bit of banter over a knick-knack. The place was empty apart from some American tourist couple who were lingering less than purposefully over a Limoges vase. Just for fun, I went over to them and told them to buy or bugger off. Marvellous!

The silly man actually asked Caroline to call the manager and have this drunken woman evicted. She trilled a peal of that laughter she does so well. I took a deep breath and let them have it. "I am not only the manager, but also the proprietress," and just then, quite by chance, I let off an enormous burp. "Furthermore, I may be drunk, but you are ugly and in the morning I shall be sober." I thought they might have recognised that, seeing as the chap who said it saved the whole of Western civilisation. Quite lost on them, but I felt hugely braced. Nothing like a bit of insult after a disturbing event in your life.

It was one of those fabulous and dreadful afternoons that you get only in England. Pervasive drizzle and the splosh of Britons wishing they were richer and thinking about strong tea. Caught the mood of it and was jolly nearly sober by the time I reached home. Can't have that, I thought. So I popped into the offie for half a dozen bottles of tonic. Thank God Hubert's taken to nipping across the Channel— saves me a fortune on spirits. He has his uses. I wonder if that'll change now. It's been a sibling relationship. Odd how sometimes you have an attraction to someone and you both think that you're going to be lovers and then you discover that you're not.

There was still a bit of grey light in the sky when I got in, but I pulled the curtains, settled myself with a humungous G&T, and had a bit of a gawp at the telly. Dreadful film on. Some knackered black-and-white thing about some femme fatale type enchanting a succession of nonstarter males. Last thing I remember was the chesty bint playing the lead cooing provocatively at some daft man. When I came to, I had a splitting headache. It was early still, because that ridiculous presenter—the tall one—was doing the news. I took a couple of asprins and washed them down with a small one. Not much of a supper.

"This won't do at all, Old Girl," I said to myself. Aloud. I always call myself "Old Girl" when attacked by loathsome self-pity. That's what my father used to call me and the memory of that alone makes me so furious that I instantly feel different. Not better, different. I couldn't fancy poaching my own eggs so I decided to trot along to the wop shop for a plate of bol and the second half of that small one. Then I made a mistake. I phoned Hubert and asked him if he wanted to rush out and join me. He told me he was busy. Extraordinary. The old fool almost never goes out alone after dark these days, least not since he encountered that chap with the adjustable spanner and got his silly head kicked in.

"But we've got things to talk about," I said.

"We can talk," said Hubert, "tomorrow?"

It doesn't do to be needy with Hubert. So I said no more and went out.

On the street passed two or three groups of youth. That is the trouble with Notting Hill, you do get them. Laughing they were, thinking themselves, what, witty? I pity them really, they'll find out. Put me in a foul mood, which was a bloody good thing because I remembered just in time that the last trip to Mario's I'd had a stand-up fight with the greasy one. Can't show mine in there for at least another month. Looked in at the Queen of Spades. That toothless oaf of a barman was on—the one that fancies me. So I left it at that. Hubert lives quite near the Queen. Funny. We used to go in there often years ago. There was singing then. I went into a phone box, picked up the receiver. Then I remembered, he'd gone out. He was busy. It was raining again. Trudged home. No appetite now. I could always have some toast at home. I wondered why I had bothered to go out.

Home again, home again, jiggety jog. There was the telephone. It felt as if it was looking at me. I mixed another drink, I wanted to. I love drinking. I love it when you say to yourself, "It's all right, I'll do it after this drink." Or, "I'll do it tomorrow." And I love the moment when you're plastered enough to know that you'll never bloody do it—whatever it is!

I stood in front of the telephone and I made it in my mind the symbol for all my crushed hopes, all my hurting. I knew then if I could pick it up and dial. . .

And I did it. I picked it up and dialed the number. Felt a rush of bravery—daft cow—it's only a telephone. There was a voice. I heard them say something. I didn't feel brave then. I couldn't speak. The pain in my throat was like a knife made of ice. I felt like one of those pathetic obscene breather people. Eventually I managed to say, "My name's Alice Hatcher." It came out softly. Had to say again. "My name's Alice Hatcher, . . . and I'm a bitter, lonely, middle-aged woman who's full of hatred."

I meant it to be a joke. But it didn't come out like that. Not funny. I was shocked awake and stone cold, because . . . I knew it was true. I wanted to put the phone down, but my hand gripped the receiver tighter. I put down the drink, and with my free hand, cut myself off. Through the window in the street a couple of student types lurched into view. Legless. One of them threw up under the lamp post. Usually, I would have yelled out something like "If you can't hold it, don't take it." He'll have a head tomorrow. Meanwhile the other one just staggered around in a circle. Reminded me of Hubert that, not even trying to help.

Oh Hubert.

I wanted to ring him then. Funnily enough, he's the only one who would have appreciated the comedy of me doing the tense tragedy queen number down the phone to some complete stranger. Mind you, I expect they're all wierdos who do that job.

No, I'd just like to get him face to face and say—I'd say, "Hubert. I've never liked you. I loved you once. And today you appear to me looking young again, and it shakes me. It's not kind. I don't know who you are, how do I know who I am?"

It was nearly dawn when I woke again. 4:30. I'd been asleep in the chair. It's a long time since I was awake at that hour. I could see a faint light in the sky. My first impulse was for another drink, because I had the dream again. But even I won't take gin at 4:30 in the morning. So there was nothing for it but to face it out sober. I decided then to ring again, because I had my dream again. In a strange way it was like seeing one of my family again, it's been so long since I had it.

I've been dreaming this dream for nearly all my grown-up life, on and off. It's always the same. I'm running, running, running away. There's someone on a motorbike chasing me. I don't know who it is. A big, a huge figure—all in shadow. Coming nearer all the time. I'm screaming and running and the motorbike is getting nearer all the time and just as it's about to catch me I wake up screaming. Terrified.

But it was different this time. This time—in the dream I turned around and stood my ground. The motorbike stopped, and the dark figure got off. I was frightened—very much so, but I didn't run. He—it was an old man—took off his helmet. Long white hair and a wrinkled face. He stepped out of his dark clothes and I saw that he was dressed all in white. He approached me, he smiled. Then he said, "Why have you been running away from me all this time? I've got something wonderful to tell you."

And that's when I woke up.

So I picked up the phone and dialed the number. I would speak this time. I needed help. As before, I heard a voice say something. But this time it was a voice I knew, it was Hubert's voice.

And he said, "Hello, Samaritans. Can I help you?"

Birth Day

Birth Day

IN THE MOMENT that they did so, Alexander felt sure that they had conceived a child. Gwynne felt so too.

They had decided to try for one a month or so beforehand, but now that it had happened, a realisation stole upon Alexander's mind: He had given the matter of what would happen next absolutely no thought whatsoever. Now was not the time to start thinking, but the seed and the egg were giving notice as one that quite a lot of thinking was going to go on in the near future. For now, the two of them smiled at each other and at the largeness of the event. A whole new person.

Gwynne phoned Roz—who had five small daughters—the next morning as soon as they had the confirmation of the testing kit.

"You're up the duff!" said Roz, not needing to be told.

"How did you know?" asked Gwynne.

"You get the feel for it after a while. Well, I knew you were trying. Let me know when you're ready, I'll give you a sack of baby clothes."

"We can't take anything yet, we've got to move first."

Alexander looked up quickly from his poached egg. He watched Gwynne at the phone. She had a biro and was onto a second page of notes.

"Right," she was saying, "Uh huh, where do I get those? . . . Okay I'll try that . . . oh yes, the NCT, I'll give them a ring today . . . no, well not yet, it was only two weeks ago last night."

Alexander blushed. Gwynne handed him the phone. "She wants a word."

"Well done, Alex," Roz trumpeted down the line. "About bloody time mind you. I'll get Steve."

"Do we have to move?" said Alexander to Gwynne.

"Darling! Of course we do, I mean where would it go?"

"Couldn't we put it in a drawer, or under the sink?"

"Alex!" said Gwynne in a way that worried him. He held out a hand, but Steve was at the other end.

"You've done it now—idiot! You free tonight?"

"Mmm?" mumbled Alexander, his focus split. "Oh, I think so."

"Not for long mate," Steve laughed. "Meet me down the Plough 'bout eight. Bloody fool!" And he hung up.

Changes happened in Alexander's life. The first flat they tried to buy fell through; the survey said it was infested with snails. When they were not looking for another place to live, they attended an Active Birth class. Alexander had considered himself to be as "New" as the next man, but when he heard other men talking happily with their partners about maternity bras, he knew that his Newness lacked real depth.

"Why have you come here, Alex?" asked Jessica, the Birth Teacher. "What do you want to get out of this course?"

"I want to know if I can have an epidural too," quipped Alexander. The instant he'd said it the room fell quiet. Under the silent regard of expectant mothers and fathers who looked at him with enlightened hostility, Alexander knew that he had committed a hideous breach of good taste. And all the while, Alexander's confusions and his joys at adjusting to his new role in life went for the most part unspoken. For the most part unacknowledged.

Once a week he went to the pub with Steve. That was more time than he would, left to his own devices, have spent with Steve, whose company he enjoyed on an occasional basis. There was strong collusion on all sides for him to go under the heading of "Getting Another Man's View." So he went, and drank.

"Stroke of luck this, for me," said Steve. "Gets me out. Brilliant. So how's it going?"

"Fine," said Alexander. "Had the first scan last week."

He remembered his confusion at seeing the indistinct image of his child. His surprise that it was possible to spy inside his wife's body like this, his disappointment at not feeling more. No rapture. No awe. He'd leant down and kissed Gwynne's tummy. Then he'd whispered into her belly "Hello. This is your father speaking. Hello."

Alexander wondered whether to talk this over with Steve. But Steve wasn't in the mood to listen. This was precious air time. "See, what you've got to remember. Right? Is that THEY are not like us."

"They?" asked Alexander.

"You know, women, THEM, the enemy. They see it differently. Now, when she's demanding cabbage and molasses, right, you've got to remember that it's just hormones. Talking of that. Know what I'm not looking forward to?"

"No," said Alexander wondering what he was doing there.

"Terribly sexist thing to say this, still I'll say it anyway. In about ten years from now, I'm going to come home one day and find that my wife and five kids are all menstruating at the same time. 'Nother pint?"

And so it went, life now numbered by weeks. Because it was their first child, congratulations were extra indulgent, women would give sunbeam smiles, men would handshake vigorously and look him in the eye. At birth class he learned to breathe deeply, he learned the rudiments of massage, and he began to worry about money.

"You've just got to go out and get some more," counselled Steve. "Don't worry you will. Red hot poker of necessity, mate. 'Nother pint?"

At sixteen weeks, they found a garden flat at a knockdown price. Inside was not a cupboard, shelf, or curtain. The estate agent, the lawyer, and the bank all assured them that the transaction was a straightforward one, and they'd be in the new home in plenty of time for the baby. The delays began. Meanwhile there was, if not a nest, then at least the feathers to be gathered for it. People came up with baby clothes, with children's books, with toys, more clothes. A cot appeared, and an old-fashioned pram. Gwynne's father opened a Post Office savings account and started it off with 500 pounds. Someone gave them a potty, saying with relish that although they wouldn't be getting to that stage for two or three years they'd be glad of it when the time came. The one-bedroom flat where they were living became a wharehouse for baby goods. Gwynne got over her morning sickness and began to breakfast on ice cream and pickles. Alexander's father-in-law offered to go over to the flat to be and inspect it. While there he blew the fuse box by searching for floor joists with a hammer and nail and instead hitting a live wire.

Alexander became used to the evasions that people use when they come close to the big stuff. When his father had died after a brief but painful illness, he had often heard the old cliché, "Perhaps it was for the best, in a way." Now he often heard, "Better make the most of your sleep while you can." And there would be a riotous laugh, which made him want to punch people. "Ever been bankrupt?" asked the mortgage broker.

"No," said Alexander.

"Soon will be," laughed the broker.

Steve was delighted when Alexander began to voice his discomfort.

"Great!" said Steve, "Excellent. I've been waiting for this. This is exactly how it's supposed to be. Total 'kin nightmare. Nature's way, mate. Let's have a short."

So Alexander settled with a picture of himself as a worker bee. Rushing busily about. All other purposes in his life now sublimated powerfully and perhaps permanently to the one great cause of ushering in the next generation, and feeding it.

And then a vet asked Gwynne a question and everything changed. The vet was a friend of a friend that they met at dinner party one night. She happened to tell a story about a neighbour's cat.

"I don't want to worry you," said the vet, "but have you been tested for toxoplasmosis?" He went on to explain that the test was not routine, but might be a good idea in view of the circumstances. Mildly alarmed, but not gravely so, Gwynne went to the hospital and requested a blood test. Both of them assumed the result would be negative. A week went by. A nurse telephoned them in some agitation. Alexander took the call. "Your wife has to see the consultant as soon as possible."

Mr. Lomax had a gentle authority. He explained carefully just what the situation was. The presence of antibodies in Gwynne's blood indicated that she had been exposed at some time to the disease. They would need to do a further blood test to establish when that exposure had been. In the meantime, she must start an immediate course of antibiotics which she must continue to term. These were preventive drugs which crossed the placenta into the growing baby and would mitigate the worst effects—if indeed there had been any effects, which no one could say for certain at this stage.

"What kind of effects, doctor?" asked Gwynne.

"Possibly quite devastating," said the consultant.

He looked at them to see how they took it. Alexander felt his face flush and the pressure of water behind his eyes; he took Gwynne's hand. Because they had to know, the consultant listed the possibilities. Alexander heard ". . . brain damage . . . loss of hearing, or vision . . . bone malformation. In another six weeks we'll be able to do a cordocentesis, which will establish with a fair degree of certainty whether the baby has been harmed."

"Is there any risk in doing that? To the baby, I mean," asked Gwynne.

"Fewer than 1 percent miscarry. And you'd have the top man in the country to do it. In the worst case," Mr Lomax went on, "you would have a choice. It would be rather late in the pregnancy, and we are all aware that the emotional consequences of that would be appalling for you."

They got home by walking slowly and holding each other's hands not talking. Practical things to occupy the mind. A prescription to be filled. Remember to pick up some more milk. Post the mortgage offer back to the building society. The question that they must face became a tangible thing almost. They couldn't decide now, but they must be ready to decide when they knew.

At the birth classes, Alexander sensed the group differently. All the parents-to-be sitting on bean bags or cushions, and all the unborn in the room quietly wanting the best. It did a lot to calm his nerves. But grateful though he was for this support, he never could bring himself to say, "We are pregnant."

At other times he was swept by passion. The natural process in his psyche where he was becoming a father, his instincts to nurture being licked alight like a slow match on damp newspaper difficult to light, this gradual process—perhaps surer because of its hesitations and reverses—was now accelerated in the pain of his urgent, desperate love for the child. The crisis broke his heart—broke it open. And he found himself faced with metaphysics and morality.

Not weeks passing now but days, long, and one at a time. When their turn for the test came, Gwynne was pale with anxiety. They watched the screen and saw the needle travel slowly down the amniotic fluid to puncture the umbilical cord and draw blood from it. It was like watching an invasion from outer space. The image was clear, their child turned its head. Now waiting for the results. Holding hands, nothing to say. "No evidence that the baby has been affected," said the consultant. Waves of relief. Release from the terrible decision. She would still have to take the drugs, eight tablets a day, and they would continue to monitor the child for two years after birth. Four months to go; sixteen weeks.

The property business stretched their sanity still further, but they got the keys three weeks to the day before the due date. Sitting at last and by now against their hopes in their new flat, their daily circular phone conversations with all the reluctant professionals forgotten for the moment, the cot assembled but still no cupboards, Gwynne felt the first contractions. "Here we go," she said.

"But the car!" said Alexander. The car was being serviced so as to be ready in time.

"Roz," said Gwynne.

Roz delivered them to the hospital. "Ring Steve when you're ready to come home," she told Alexander.

All through the afternoon they practised the breathing exercises together. They yelled together as the pain increased. About supper time there was a change of shifts, the new midwife arrived, and suddenly the room was filled with people ready to take samples and read monitors—this birth must be recorded because of the toxoplasmosis scare. Among them was a keen young doctor, a convert to the idea of birth without drugs.

"I don't know how much more I can take," said Gwynne. Alexander was relieved, knowing that she had already taken more than he could have. "Too late!" said the young doctor cheerfully. "She's in second stage. Isn't it wonderful? You're doing it naturally—just like you wanted!"

He was referring to the birth plan that they had written in a time of high enthusiasm at the birth classes. Alexander had a picture of himself felling the man with a right cross as though in a scene from a television sitcom. Instead, he grabbed the doctor's arm. "How long?!" he demanded.

"About twenty minutes I should think," said the doctor, puzzled.

Alexander yelled in his wife's ear, "Hear that? Twenty minutes."

Gwynne looked at him, managed a smile, then the next contraction came.

"That's it." It was the midwife. "Push this baby out. I can see the head."

The baby was born, given a little oxygen, cleaned, wrapped up, and handed to the father to hold. It was an awesome moment, but he was too tired to know what he felt. After the stitches, one of the students made Gwynne a cup of tea. "This is the best tea in the world," she said.

When he left, Gwynne and the baby were sleeping. Alexander called Steve.

"Result!" said Steve. "Definite result! Mind you, I was worried. I thought, 'He's cutting this a bit fine.' Still, I think we'll make it, it's only quarter to. I'll pick you up at the gate."

They stood at the bar and Steve said, "Ugly little things when they first come out, aren't they?"

Then Alexander knew what he had felt as he'd held his baby in his arms for the first time, its angry prune head looking up at him. He'd felt as if he were watched by one of the many faces of God.

Cold Call
A Thirty-Minute Radio Play

Cold Call
A Thirty-Minute Radio Play

The action takes place in the sales offices of Radical Moves Publications. RMP is a publishing company that sells advertising space to anyone who will stay on the phone long enough to hear a sales pitch.

CHARACTERS

Philip Swift, a telephone salesman new to the job. Hard-up novelist.

Sylvie, his boss, general sales manager at RMP

Karen, joint managing director of the Stationery Factory

Greg, super-aggressive star salesperson at RMP

Harvey, not very good at selling. Low-energy salesman.

Receptionists, Managing Directors, Chairpeople, Company Executive Officers

SCENE 1

Monday morning. The sales floor of RMP. There are over a hundred people working here. They are constantly on the phone. We hear a background of animated sales pitches, expletives when people are cut off, and the savage banter that goes with this work. Three times in the whole play there is a cry of triumph as confirmation is received by fax that some business somewhere in the world has agreed to part with thousands to purchase a full page in colour. It is Philip's first day.

Philip: Er . . . Hi. 'Scuse me, is Sylvie around?

Greg: Who wants to know?

Philip: Oh yes. I'm Philip. Swift. Philip Swift.

Greg: Just finished training?

Philip: Yes.

Greg: What are you, Phil?

Philip: Sorry?

Greg: Never apologise Phil. First rule of sales.

Philip: Oh, sorry. No. Er, right.

Greg: So . . . ? Out-of-work actor? Student? Redundant merchant banker?

Philip: Writer. I suppose.

Greg: You don't know?

Philip: Mmm?

Greg: What, journalism?

Philip: No, novels.

Greg: Aha. Best-sellers.

Philip: Not yet.

Greg: Good job for you this. Sell this, sell anything—you with me?

Philip: Totally.

Greg: Great team here Phil. You'll make a lot of money. Do yourself a favour, Phil. Try and get one in quickly. That's the way to make your name in the company. At the end of the day, that's what we're here for.

Philip: Sure. Is Sylvie . . . ?

Greg: That's her over there. Just closing one for Harvey—see, she's on the extension—all the phones here have got one. Means she can hear what the punter's saying, and tell you what to say.

Philip: Can the punters hear her?

Greg: 'Course not. That's the point. She can listen to them—mind you, she doesn't usually bother to listen to what the punters are coming out with—waste of time. She's brilliant. Pluck a sale out of nothing.

Philip: I see.

Greg: She could sell damp matches in the rain, Sylvie. He's a sad bastard, Harvey. (*Shouts*) Harvey, you sad bastard!

SCENE 2

Sylvie is dictating to Harvey who is trying unsuccessfully to relay what she says to Dieter, the managing director of Saxony Beers. Sylvie and Harvey's lines should overlap.

Harvey: But Dieter, *Hotel International* goes to all the purchasing managers throughout Europe. . . .

Sylvie: (*On the earpiece*) Which mean that . . . which means that——

Dieter: I have said no to you three times Mr. Harvey, don't make me put the phone down.

Sylvie: Which means that Saxony Beer will be seen as the natural supplier to all the purchasers.

Harvey: Which means that Saxony Beer——

Dieter: We are not interested.

Harvey: ——will be seen as the natural supplier for all the hotels.

Sylvie: Purchasers!

Harvey: Er, purchasers.

Dieter: You know why we don't advertise in this kind of publication?

Harvey: No. Why?

Sylvie: If you had an order from the Ritz chain of hotels . . .
Harvey: If you had an——
Dieter: Because it doesn't work.
Harvey: ——order from the Ritz . . .
Sylvie: Would you be able to supply on an continental basis?
Dieter: Everybody in the hotels are far too busy to read your
    publication.
Harvey: Could you supply internationally?
Dieter: It is a complete waste of money.
Sylvie: So can I go ahead and book a page for you?
Harvey: So can I go ahead——
Dieter: I am too busy now.
Harvey: Oh, well look . . . can I ring you after lunch?
Sylvie: Moron.
Dieter: Yes, of course.
Sylvie: Are you serious about getting that new business next
    year?
Dieter: Good luck, Mr. Harvey.
Harvey: Thank you, Dieter.
Sylvie: SAY WHAT I'M SAYING!
Harvey: Say what I'm saying.
Dieter: Good-bye, Mr. Harvey.

    Click.

Sylvie: When I'm dictating to you Harvey, you say EXACTLY
    what I tell you. Right?
Harvey: Okay, Sylvie.
Sylvie: You just lost that order.
Harvey: He wasn't going to——
Sylvie: You let him go!
Harvey: No, I didn't.
Sylvie: I heard you do it. "Can I ring you after lunch?"
Harvey: He said I could.
Sylvie: You'll never get through to him again. I've told you.

When you get through to the decision maker, DON'T LET THEM GO!!!

Harvey: But how could I . . . ?

Sylvie: Talk about golf . . . sex . . . Christmas . . . anything.

Harvey: Oh, okay.

Greg: Harvey, you are a sad man. Sylvie, this is Phil. He's starting today.

Sylvie: Welcome to the boiler room, Phil.

Philip: Thanks. Hi.

Sylvie: Hear that just now?

Philip: Yes.

Sylvie: Example of how not to do it. Right. At the beginning, so's you know. I expect upward of ten full pitches a day, and don't spend all your time in the smoking room.

Philip: Right.

Sylvie: And benefits. All the time. Which means that . . . for your company. Which means that . . . lots of lovely new business. Which means that . . . a huge increase in your sales.

Philip: Right.

Sylvie: And remember.

Philip: What?

Sylvie: They have to like you. They'll buy you before they buy advertising. You've either got it or you haven't in this game, and you've definitely got it Phil.

SCENE 3

The hubbub of telephone solicitation percolates in the background. The impression is one of energised calling. The sales staff are attempting to communicate the good news. It is Philip's first call. He is hesitant.

Harvey: Nervous?

Philip: No. Just wondering how to begin.

Harvey: Don't worry, it gets worse.

Greg: It's a great call this one. Your first time live. Could be the one. Who you calling?

Philip: Manufacturer of cruet sets.

Greg: Fantastic. Huge market for that. They'll bite your hand off.

   Philip dials. Ringing tone.

Receptionist: Hello, Pepperpot.

Philip: Pepperpot?

Receptionist: Pepperpot.

Philip: Could I speak to the managing director please?

Receptionist: Who's calling?

Philip: Philip Swift.

Receptionist: From?

Philip: From the League of Luxury Hotels—well, on behalf of——

Receptionist: Is it advertising?

Philip: Er, er——

Receptionist: Not interested.

   Click.

Greg: Blow you out did she? Ring back with a different name. Say you're the president of the European Board of Trade. Go on.

Philip: Seriously?

Greg: Seriously. Look, tell them you're the Pope if you want. Just get through.

   Philip dials. Ringing.

Receptionist: Pepperpot.

Philip: European Board of Trade calling for the managing
    director.
Receptionist: Go away!

Click.

SCENE 4

*The end of Philip's first day. The background is less animated
now. People are winding down. A shout of triumph as one of
Greg's deals comes up on the board. Shouts of "Nice one, Greg,"
"Well done," "Brilliant," and so on.*

Greg: Sorted! That's my Portuguese construction company.
    Had to give them a discount. Still, I'll take ten percent
    of that. How's it going your end Phil?
Philip: Not bad. Not too good. I can't get through most of
    the time.
Greg: Come and have a smoke.
Philip: Oh I don't—not anymore.
Greg: You can't sell if you don't smoke, mate. It's all right,
    I've got some.

SCENE 5

*In the smoking room. The background is muted through a parti-
tion wall. Occasionally the door opens and we hear the phone
lines buzzing more distinctly.*

Philip: It's like being inside an ashtray.
Greg: Yeah, they don't want you in here too long. Now look,
    these secretaries, don't tell them anything.
Philip: But when they ask you what you're calling about,
    what do you say?
Greg: Don't say anything.

Philip: You've got to say something.

Greg: They start getting above themselves. Try to tell you you want the marketing director and rubbish like that.

Philip: Oh. I've got a question. Suppose they want to see a copy of the publication.

Greg: I'd be delighted—always be delighted—delighted to send you the magazine. Then, before they get thinking about it—straight onto something totally different. Tell me, your cutlery, is it plate or are you using new technology? Did you see Helmut Kohl on telly last night? Get them talking to you. They're not going to spend five and a half grand with you if you don't chat them up.

Philip: "Light on the objections, strong on the benefits."

Greg: That's it! It's a beautiful thing—a sale. It's like fishing. Get the hook in there. Appeal to their greed, give them plenty of line. Then gently, gently, just reel them in. Play it right, you've got them asking you. And always ask for the business. Don't ask—you don't get.

Philip: Right.

Greg: Now, when you come in tomorrow, say to yourself, "Today's the day."

SCENE 6

Tuesday morning, Philip's second day. Strong background.

Sylvie: Come on, Philip. Should have been on the phone by now. Come on, Europe's been in the office for an hour already.

Greg: What are you saying to yourself today, Phil?

Philip: Today's the day, Greg.

Greg: That's it! Get out there and dial. Want to see you get through sixty to eighty calls today.

Sylvie: I need you to get aggressive today, Philip. Now, when

you're through to the right person, push them. That's
the job.

Philip: Okay.

Sylvie: You're not here to make friends. Get them excited.

Philip dials. The phone rings.

Receptionist: Torvoldson Ice.

Philip: Is Mr. Torvoldson the managing director?

Receptionist: He is the chairman.

Philip: Yes, of course. Could I speak with him please?

Torvoldson: Jacob Torvoldson.

Philip: I'm Philip Swift, calling from the League of Luxury
Hotels. We are doing an enormous amount of research
and putting together a sourcing publication which will
be the official business-to-business communication
organ throughout the industry. It goes by name and
title to all the senior management and purchasing officers throughout the entire hotel industry in Europe
and indeed worldwide. (*Silence*) Mr. Torvoldson?

Torvoldson: Yes?

Philip: We are planning to complement the editorial material with a limited number of strategic advertising po-
sitions from world-class companies like yourselves.
Now, we can communicate your message to the central purchasing offices of all the hotel chains.

Sylvie: (*Passing by*) Go for it Philip. Which means that . . .
Greg! What's happening with the Czech loo roll people?

Greg: Chomping for it, Sylv.

Philip: Which means that with your advertisement on the
opening right-hand page in the chapter on . . . (*He checks
his details*) er, ice suply, your company will be perceived
as the natural problem solver to the questions raised
in the articles about . . . er, ice . . . er, supply.

Silence.

Philip: Mr. Torvoldson?

Torvoldson: Yes?

Philip: I thought you'd gone.

Torvoldson: No.

Philip: Tell me, Mr. Torvoldson, what are your plans to, er, make ice. . . . I mean, are you going on . . . on with ice?

Torvoldson: Yes.

Philip: Fantastic! Great. Well, do you play golf?

Torvoldson: No.

Philip: Do you have sex?

Torvoldson: Yes.

Philip: Do you believe in Father Christmas?

Torvoldson: No.

Philip: And finally, do you ever say anything except yes or no?

Torvoldson: Yes.

Sylvie: (*From across the office*) Ask for the order. Go on, you haven't done that yet. Now, Maltese Glassware?

Greg: Desperate to get involved.

Philip: Terrific, Mr. Torvoldson. So look, what I'll do is get my people to fax you an order form straightaway so that we can block that space off for you and none of your competitors can get it. How does that sound?

Torvoldson: No. Goodbye.

  Click.

Sylvie: Well?

Philip: He's gone.

Sylvie: I'm worried Phil. Tell me that you are a winner.

Philip: I am. I am.

SCENE 7

Wednesday morning. The usual background.

Greg: Nice and early, Phil. Excellent. Want to see you standing on top of the desk today. Wave your arms around—
 gives you that edge.

Harvey: You do it your way, Philip.

Greg: But don't do it his way. Harvey hasn't had a deal yet
 this quarter.

Philip: Oh dear.

Greg: Go for it today, Phil. Oi Harvey! Phil's going to sell—
 before the end of the week.

Harvey: Could do.

Sylvie: Come on, boys. On the blower. Get some serious deals
 in today. Expecting something from you, Philip. Middle
 of your first week—pressure's on.

Philip dials.

Receptionist: Bloom Lighting.

Philip: Could you tell me who your M. D. is please?

Receptionist: Mr. Barfleet.

Philip: (*Pleasantly surprised*) Oh. Could I speak to Mr. Barfleet
 please? Listen—do I know you?

Receptionist: I'll put you through.

Philip: Thanks.

Secretary: Mr. Barfleet's office.

Philip: Hello? Weren't we just—Mr. Barfleet please.

Secretary: Who's calling?

Philip: I'm the senior executive of the League of Luxury
 Hotels. My name's Swift.

Secretary: In what connection?

Philip: Just put me through, will you?

Greg: Go on, Phil.

Secretary: Mr. Barfleet doesn't take calls unless he knows
 what it's about.

Philip: Mr. Barfleet will not thank you for losing him millions of quid's worth of business. Now, put me through!

Barfleet: Barfleet.

Philip: Swift here. Philip Swift. You do lights?

Barfleet: That's what we do.

Philip: Can you supply to Europe?

Barfleet: We can do anything.

Philip: Fantastic. We've been commissioned by the League of Luxury Hotels to present to them the top three or four companies—

Barfleet: What's it called? Your magazine?

Philip: Er, *Hotel International*.

Barfleet: What does it cost me?

Philip: We'll talk about price soon. You see, we go in front of a focused target audience—

Barfleet: How much?

Philip: Five thousand five hundred pounds.

Barfleet: (*Roaring with laughter*) Ridiculous—as I'm sure you know. For that sort of money I could mailshot all the buyers with my catalogue, ring them all up, and take most of them to dinner.

Philip: Well, I've just come from a meeting with Ms. Carmen Hondura, the senior buyer for the Marriot Hotels—

Barfleet: Who is a personal friend of mine . . .

Philip: Oh really. What's she like?

Barfleet: Right, lad, I think we know where we stand. We've got a lot of work to do here today, do stop ringing us up on the phone—there's a good chap.

Click.

SCENE 8

Thursday morning. Philip's fourth day.

Greg: Day four, Phil. This is it! Go for it. Pull out all the stops. Got my Hungarian fruiterer confirmed this morning. Seventeen and a half percent for me—very nice too.

Philip: I thought it was twelve and a half percent.

Greg: Ah well, I've broken into the next incentive bracket. Done a hundred and ten grand's worth this quarter. Only got to sell as much again in the next four weeks and I'm into the bonus accelerator.

Philip: Will it do them any good? The Hungarians?

Greg: Come on! They've just done a bit of business with the West—i.e., me. Good experience, that.

Philip: But will it bring them any new orders?

Greg: Get real, Phil. Luckily, that's not our problem.

Philip: But they've just spent five grand.

Greg: Ten. Got them for two issues.

Philip: Ten grand!

Greg: They don't even have to pay till after we publish.

Philip: Maybe they won't.

Greg: Ah no. Well, then we'd sue them.

Sylvie: Come on, break it up. Let's see some action. Keen today, Philip?

Philip: Hold me back, Sylvie. Here I go.

Philip dials.

Receptionist: Golden Tapp Bathrooms.

Philip: Hello?

Receptionist: Hello?

Philip: I know you.

Receptionist: No. Perhaps you think you do.

Philip: I spoke to you yesterday.

Receptionist: I don't think so.

Philip: And the day before.

Receptionist: Impossible. I'm new here. Today's my first day.

Philip: Oh. Well, the managing director please.

Receptionist: Transferring you.

Tapp: Hallo.

Philip: Good morning. Philip Swift here from the League of Luxury Hotels.

Tapp: David Tapp from Golden Tapp Bathrooms.

Philip: Brilliant.

Tapp: We like it.

Philip: If I could show you how to get Golden Tapp Bathroom fittings into hotels across Europe, would you be interested?

Tapp: Oh, of course we would.

Philip: Well it's a very good thing that I called because . . .

Greg: I think he's got one, Sylv. He's been on the phone for about half an hour. Done it brilliantly. Lots of benefits, all that lovely getting involved in the punter's life, and closing well too.

Sylvie: About time. It's often the same with these intellectual types. Sound articulate enough, but they haven't got the guts for the Big Deal.

Philip: Great, David, so can I book that page for you right now?

Tapp: I'll just have a word with my Dad.

Philip: What?!

Tapp: Yes, it's up to him, anything like that. Give us a call in a month or two. Lovely talking to you, Philip. If I were looking for a salesperson—which I'm not—you'd have a job tomorrow. Anyway—bye now.

   Click.

Greg: What happened there?

Philip: He's got to talk to his dad.

Sylvie: What!!! You spent half an hour pitching to a non-decision maker? No. I don't believe it.

Greg: Total waste of time, Phil.

Sylvie: Didn't you check?

Philip: Same name Sylvie—father and son you see.

Sylvie: Give me strength.

Greg: You can always pitch a junior. Because—it's not their money. He'll go to his dad and put your fantastic pitch into three words: "geyser selling advertising." And his dad'll say, "No."

Philip: Yeah, I think I've got that.

Sylvie: Now I am worried, Philip.

SCENE 9

Friday morning.

Sylvie: Come on, Philip. Animated pitching as if it really matters—which it does. Put a bit of snap into it.

Philip dials. The phone rings.

Karen: The Stationery Factory.

Philip: Hi! Good morning.

Karen: Hello.

Philip: Could I speak to your managing director please?

Karen: Well, I suppose you're speaking to her.

Philip: Are you sure?

Karen: Yes. I can be quite definite about that.

Philip: Terrific.

Karen: Is it?

Philip: Ah . . .

Greg: Go on, congratulate them.

Philip: Yes, it's fantastic.

Karen: Oh I am pleased. So, how can I help?

Philip: Oh yes. Er, my name's Philip Swift, and I'm calling—

Karen: Nice to meet you. My name's Karen.

Philip: And I'm Philip.

Karen: You're not going to sell me something are you?

Philip: Oh no. Not at all.

Karen: Thank goodness for that. We get so many.

Philip: That is . . . yes.

Karen: Oh what a shame. And we were getting on so well.

Philip: Well, it's my job.

Karen: I understand. Someone's got to do it.

Philip: Yes, I suppose someone has. Tell me, I understand that you are a well-respected supplier of stationery.

Karen: Now you'll have guessed that from the name of the company. The Stationery Factory.

Philip: It's a clue.

Karen: Very impressive. Very sharp. Now you're going to go into the pitch I suppose.

Philip: That would be the next step in the normal course of things.

Karen: Well don't let me stop you. Just don't be surprised if I'm not here at the end of it.

Philip: Oh, I'm used to that.

Karen: Oh dear.

Philip: I'm trying not to take it personally.

Karen: So give it a whirl then.

Philip: Shall I?

Karen: Oh go on.

Philip: Right. Good morning! You don't know me from a bar of soap, but a little thing like that is not going to stop me trying to sell you something you don't remotely need at a price that is far higher than anything you could reasonably expect to pay for a strikingly similar product elsewhere.

Karen: Yes, par for the course.

Philip: You're still there.

Karen: I like your voice.

Philip: I like yours.

Karen: It's not something our company does, to tell you the truth. We've never advertised. What happens now?

Philip: I'm supposed to ask you about your product, or get involved in your life somehow.

Karen: All right.

Philip: Do you have any plans to expand into Europe next year?

Karen: No.

Philip: What new lines are you developing?

Karen: None.

Philip: What is your best-selling item?

Karen: There isn't one.

Philip: Ah, right . . .

Karen: Try another tack.

Philip: Er, er . . .

Karen: Better pull something out, Philip. Otherwise, enchanting as this has been, I'll have to go and wash my hair.

Philip: Oh, okay . . . er, who's your favourite poet?

Karen: I'll tell you if you'll tell me.

Philip: It's a deal.

Sylvie: Deal? Is there a deal on?

Philip: Kind of.

Sylvie: Right. Easy does it. Benefits—"which mean that"—for your company. And a bit of IMI.

Philip: IMI?

Karen: Who's IMI?

Sylvie: Informed Market Information.

Karen: Is there a collected works?

Sylvie: (*On the earpiece*) So should I book you a whole page or just half—which is better for you?

Philip: Which is best for you?

Karen: Walt Whitman.

Philip: Ah, Walt Whitman . . .

Sylvie: Who as I'm sure you know is the senior manager at the central purchasing office of Ritz Carlton Hotels.

Philip: Who was the greatest manager—

Karen: —of nineteenth-century American Romantic Mysticism.

Sylvie: Now, Mr. Whitman has told us . . .

Philip: And Whitman has told us . . .

Sylvie: That there'll be a huge need for—(*whispers*) whatever she does—next year . . .

Karen: That the physical exists as token of the spiritual.

Sylvie: So you really must be seen in this publication.

Philip: So one really must see his publications.

Karen: *Leaves of Grass.*

Philip: "Song of Myself."

Sylvie: *Hotel International*! I've got a good feeling about this, Phil.

Philip: I've got a good feeling about this . . .

Sylvie: Don't say that.

Karen: You don't say . . .

Greg: Sylvie! Got one here. German interior designer, wants a page. Okay, Hans, now this is something you definitely want to go ahead with? . . . Right. Let's deal.

Sylvie: Right, Hans, what I can do for you . . .

Greg: Now what I can do for you, Hans, come aboard for two editions and I'll knock off fifteen percent . . .

Karen: Where were we, Phil?

Sylvie: Just keep her on the phone, Phil. Don't let her go.

Karen: Is it high-pressure sales where you are?

Philip: You could say that.

Karen: Take me through it then. Paint me the picture.

Philip: It's a curious set up. I'm in an office with about a hundred and twenty people. There's comfortable enough room for about sixty. We've all got phones. Each phone has an extra earpiece.

Karen: So people can listen in?

Philip: Yes.

Karen: Very Big Brother. Is anyone listening now?

Philip: Not just now.

Karen: Let me know if they do.

Philip: You'll be able to tell.

Karen: Because you'll go into sales talk?
Philip: That's right.
Karen: Why are you doing this?
Philip: Why does anyone do anything?
Karen: Fair point.
Philip: I'm not a natural salesman. I don't think so anyway.
Karen: Based upon our brief acquaintance, I'm inclined to agree with you.
Philip: I thought I ought to make some attempt to come to terms with the commercial world.
Karen: Is that a new thing?
Philip: Yes. Until now I've earned my living working in the back end of cafes or swinging paint brushes—I've been a wine waiter.
Karen: How long have you been doing this?
Philip: This is day five.
Karen: How long will you stay?
Philip: I've told myself that I must stay until I sell something.
Karen: And who knows when that may be?
Philip: Today's the day—that's what I tell myself.
Karen: Every day?
Philip: So far.
Karen: And one day your number is bound to come up.
Philip: Well, put like that, I'm sure you're right.
Karen: So what was your previous life? The one that was so uncommercial?
Philip: I was a writer.
Karen: Of poetry?
Philip: No, prose.
Karen: Articles? Stories? Features?
Philip: Novels.
Karen: How many novels?
Philip: Two unfinished, and one I'm planning—
Karen: —but can't afford to write.
Philip: Exactly.

Karen: Is it autobiographical?

Philip: Only to the extent that all writing is. No, not consciously.

Karen: What's it about?

Philip: It's about someone who thinks he's gone mad.

Karen: Ah. How many of us could say that, I wonder.

Philip: Yes. I'm interested to know why here why now?

Karen: Cast adrift in the trackless wastes of time, what particularity creates each individual fate?

Philip: That's it!

Karen: There's less room in commerce for this kind of thing than is popularly imagined.

Philip: I believe you're right there.

Karen: Take stationery, you see. We almost never bother with the deeper mysteries when we take our products to market. Does that surprise you?

Philip: I can't honestly say it does.

Karen: Do you know, neither can I. So there we have it. Our approach has been completely sensible. Perhaps that's where we've gone wrong.

Philip: But you're still in business.

Karen: Yes. Possibly not for a great while longer.

Philip: Oh I'm sorry to hear that. Is business falling off?

Karen: No, no the company's doing rather well in fact.

Philip: Oh, that's good. Why do you think—

Karen: Oh, sometimes you just get a feeling about these things.

Philip: An intuition?

Karen: I think you'll find that Jung separates the functions of feeling and intuition. They are quite distinct.

Philip: Of course, I was forgetting.

Karen: Talking of Jung—

Philip: —as one does—

Karen: This is a synchronicitous telephone call.

Philip: It is?

Karen: Indeed so.

Philip: Say more.

Karen: How long would it take you to write your novel? Working nine to five, that is.

Philip: Six months.

Karen: And how much money would you need to keep body and soul together for that time?

Philip: Maybe a thousand a month. Then I wouldn't have to worry about anything else.

Karen: More would be welcome, I take it.

Philip: Anything would be.

Karen: Now I've got some questions for you.

Philip: Fire away.

Karen: Your magazine is called?

Philip: *Hotel International*.

Karen: Published?

Philip: Quarterly.

Karen: A page costs?

Philip: Five and a half grand.

Karen: Double page?

Philip: Nine and a half.

Karen: Back cover?

Philip: Seven and a half.

Karen: What's your cut?

Philip: Ten percent on a page, twelve and a half on anything above that, seventeen and a half on everything in any one week where I sell more than two and a half pages.

Karen: I see. . . . Hang on a sec.

Sylvie: (*Coming over*) Greg, how did that happen—don't tell me you're losing your touch. Can't anybody here sell space!? Come on, Philip, it's not therapy you're giving her. Let's have a listen.

Karen: It seems to me, Philip, that if someone booked a page, a double page, and a back cover for each of the quarterly issues for the next year, then your commission would be seventeen and a half percent of 84,000 pounds. That is 15,750 pounds before tax. Is that correct?

Philip: I'm sure it is, if you say so. How did you—

Karen: I'm naturally arithmetic.

Philip: Yes, well, as you say, that would be the sort of thing to aim at.

Karen: And then the novel could be written?

Philip: Yes it could.

Sylvie: Tell her we'll knock fifteen percent off on a multiple order.

Philip: We'll knock fifteen percent off.

Karen: Someone's on the earpiece?

Philip: My boss.

Sylvie: And another five percent if she pays up front.

Philip: And five percent more if you pay up front.

Karen: I'm not interested in the discounts.

Philip: You're not?

Karen: That would ruin your commission.

Philip: What?!

Karen: Fax me the order form now, would you?

Philip: What?! Are you sure? I mean—

Karen: Yes, I'm quite decided. I think this is just what the company needs.

Sylvie: This is a wind up. She's never going to sign a form for eighty-four grand's worth.

Karen: I'm absolutely serious. If I receive a fax within the next two minutes, I shall sign it and return it immediately.

Sylvie: You never know. Right. Is this the fax number?

Philip: Yes.

Sylvie: Keep her talking. CLEAR THE FAX MACHINE!!!

The office background dies down. Everyone listens to Philip.

Karen: There is a condition, Philip.

Philip: (*His mouth has gone dry*) Yes?

Karen: On receipt of my order, in fact directly we have finished our conversation, you will leave that office and
never go back.

Philip: (*Repeating mechanically*) You want me to leave this
job once you've placed your order?

Sylvie: Tell her whatever she wants to hear, we're not letting
you go, Phil, you're a star. Best salesman we've had in years.
Long as you don't sign anything, she can't touch you.

Karen: I'll have that in writing, Philip.

Philip: Where do I sign?

Karen: No, I'll take your word. I know you'll keep the bargain.

Philip: I'm flattered.

Karen: Ah here it comes now. I'll sign it directly and send it
back.

Philip: Just one question.

Sylvie: (*Hissing*) Not yet. Don't jinx it.

Philip: You are just about to spend a very great deal of
money—

Karen: I've spent it already, should be with you any second.

Philip: But why?

Sylvie: I don't believe it! Here it comes. She's signed it!
  Massive cheers, big reaction from the office.

Karen: Is there something happening at your end?

Philip: This is not something we see every day, Karen.

Sylvie: Greg!

Greg: Yes, Sylvie?

Sylvie: Get off your backside and get out there and buy me
a bottle of champagne for our star. No. Get a case!

Karen: Good luck with literature, Philip.

Sylvie: Philip, give her the spiel; welcome to the publication, blah, blah—then get off the phone.

Philip: Welcome to the publication—

Karen: Don't bother with the spiel.

Philip: Right. Look, perhaps we could—dinner? The opera?
A soccer match? Whatever you like . . .

Karen: No, I don't think so Philip—thank you for asking. Oh, shall I tell you why? I think you wanted to know that.

Philip: Yes.

Karen: It's quite simple. My husband told me that he was going on a business trip. He asked me to man the phones while he was away.

Philip: Oh.

Karen: Exactly a week ago this morning, I discovered a receipt for two first-class aeroplane tickets to the Canary Islands. The secretary who was supposed to be off sick is not at home. A telephone call to the Grand Hotel connected me with my husband going by the name of Mr. Smith.

Philip: Ah.

Karen: I have also managed to sell the house, the car, and the collection of miniature cottages. They were all in my name for tax purposes anyway.

Philip: I see.

Karen: Still, I'm sure he'll think it's been worth it. He did make a point of asking me to make sure that all the bills were paid.

The Kite

The Kite

IN THE WAITING ROOM Fred gazed at a pile of magazines.

"Alfred Brown."

The nurse's voice sounded efficient. He stood up and tried to smile.

"In here," said the nurse. "Mr. Twaites will see you now."

Fred felt a stab in his chest. He knew it wasn't the nurse's fault, but he always felt that pain when people told him what to do. The consultant's room was a brightly lit box of a place with a desk where the consultant sat. There were no magazines. Fred sat down.

"It's bad news I'm afraid," said Mr. Twaites. "We've got the results of your electrocardiogram, and it is very much as we feared."

Fred heard the consultant speaking as though from a long way off; he couldn't hear the words, just the plummy vowels of an educated voice. It was a sound which Fred at once respected and despised. Mr. Twaites scribbled on a prescription pad, and handed a leaf to Fred.

"Come back and see us in three months. This should help with the pain."

"Thank you, doctor."

• • •

At home Irene had started already. "What'd they say then?" she asked.

"Gimme some more pills."

"Blimey. It's like a chemists in here."

"Any dinner?" asked Fred, inoffensively quiet.

"Go up the chip shop when they open," said Irene.

The stab in the heart; he caught his breath. He smiled. "Shall I get some for you?"

"I don't want none." She took another sip.

"What about Ricky?"

"Yeah, he'll need feeding. Mick rang. Says he's coming to see you tonight. What's he want?"

"I don't know. I haven't seen him in more than a year. We'll go down the pub."

"You better, I don't want him in my house again."

• • •

The two brothers sat in the saloon bar of The Hand & Flower over two pints of stout.

"How's the old bag?"

"Don't, Mick. Don't call her that. She likes you really."

"She hates my guts. She knows I'd have had you out of her clutches years ago if it weren't for Ricky."

Mick looked at his brother and wondered which of them had had the harder life. He knew his own had been more adventurous than Fred's. He thought, irrationally, of lobster thermidor in Paris; and then, by association of opposites, of the greasy tea in Wandsworth prison. He wished his brother would fight back, but Fred was still, and always had been, a mouse.

"Oh don't go all quiet on me. Listen Fred, I've got something I want you to do. Something I want you to try for me."

"I'm not doing any thieving."

"No. Nothing like that, that's all over years ago. Listen to me. I want you to go and see someone. A kind of doctor. A psychotherapist."

"I've got a heart condition. I'm not mental."

"Just try it, Fred. Humour me."

"Have you been to one?"

"Yes." Mick grinned, a sly look came over his features as though he were confessing a fetish. "When I came out of the nick and broke up with Molly, I went a bit wobbly."

Fred swallowed some beer and chuckled, "You were off the wall."

"Yes I was. Look, that's not the point is it? The point is you've got to go. I've told this woman you're coming."

"Woman! I don't want to see a woman doctor."

"Why not? She's not going to take your clothes off."

Mick knew that wasn't strictly accurate. He remembered the time he first understood that he was a teenager who had never grown up. Walking out of that session, he had felt completely naked. He went on, "It can change things, Freddie. Look at me. There's a lot of things I don't do any more."

The money might have been a problem, but Mick had it covered. He would pay for it, for a year anyway.

"A year!" It was the closest Fred had ever come to shouting at his brother.

"Takes time, Fred."

In the end Fred agreed; he couldn't resist. He was touched that Mick cared so much about him, but he felt more stabbing pain in his chest, smothered jealousy that Mick could control other people's lives when he couldn't control anything.

• • •

Gillian Hoff lived in a double-fronted victorian house covered in ivy overlooking a park. Fred had never been inside a house like it. The room where they sat and talked was painted pale green, Fred sat on a sofa and Gillian in a cushioned swivel chair. Coloured light came across an old and overgrown garden. She wore blouses with bright floral patterns on them. At first it was bitter to sit in comfort opposite this woman so assured who asked him personal questions. What brought Fred back in the early sessions was that she seemed to like him. More than that, it was as if she found him and the fact that he was alive valuable, as if the world were better off for Fred's existence. A bit at a time Gillian Hoff heard the story of Fred's life.

Fred and his brother had been raised by their mother; his father had been a sailor in the Merchant Navy and often away at sea. His mother had been a tough woman—even the local dustmen were frightened of her (she had once knocked one unconscious in a fistfight). Fred said his younger brother had been born with all the brains and all the charm; it was always Mick who would manage to calm her rages. At school it was Mick who was the popular one, the clever one.

When the boys were teenagers, Mick began to bring things home. First a clock, then some new saucepans. Sometimes food. But Fred never brought anything home and he felt a failure. Fred was always feeling a failure. From school he went straight to work in the paper factory at the end of the street. His job there had been the same since the first day and had taken him five minutes to learn. It was to pull a lever to release stabilizer into the pulp.

When Gillian Hoff asked him how he felt about his job, Fred's first answer was, "It's all right." The next time she asked he surprised himself: "I hate it." Fred had hated that job for three decades.

He had met Irene in the public bar of The Hand & Flower. She was playing darts. When Gillian took him back to that moment, Fred recalled the smoke and the noise. Irene was the centre of attention, throwing darts and making big scores, winning matches for the team. How the room went quiet before she threw and exploded when she scored well.

How beautiful she had looked. "I thought she was like my mother," Fred told Gillian.

They had married about two years later. She had been Mick's girl. But Mick was moving out of the area, getting to know big-time villains, succeeding in crime. Soon Mick was too important to bother with a local girl like Irene the darts player. Fred said that she married him to spite Mick, and to tear the brothers apart.

When Ricky was born, they had been married ten years. By the time he was a year old, they knew he would never walk without a stick. Two years ago Fred had gone to the doctors for the pains in his chest, which were getting stronger. Tablets, more tablets, eventually the specialist and the electrocardiogram. "I'm afraid you're heading for a heart attack, old chap." At times Fred would stop talking.

"What is it Fred?" Gillian asked when it first happened. "Do you have pain?"

He nodded.

"Where?"

He tapped his chest.

"When there are situations which are too hurtful to face, we bury the pain. If as a child you needed to cry, and to be loved, and those needs were not met, the child in you still has those needs. The pain has not changed, it has not gone away."

But Fred would not cry.

• • •

"Fred, let's try something different today. Lie down. Close your eyes."

With suggestion she relaxed him. She questioned him, leading him slowly into his subconscious, at last asking, "Was there ever a time Fred, when your heart was in it? When your heart was light?"

From behind his closed eyes, Fred was astonished to see himself as a little boy aged nine or ten, walking up a slope with his father. His dad was carrying a kite. Then he saw how, when the kite was high in the air, his dad turned to him and handed him the spindle. "You fly it son." Fred felt again that rush of pleasure through his whole body, how his body felt turned to sunlight, how suddenly fresh all the colours had seemed. He remembered too, how for a long time afterward he would see his dad turning to him with the spindle.

"You know," Fred said, "it sounds silly," and Gillian was alert.

"It sounds silly, but when I used to fly a kite."

"When was that Fred?"

"I was about ten. With my dad. It was the one thing he taught me how to do. When he was away at sea I used to practise, so that when he came back and asked me how my kite was going, I'd say, it's really great dad, and he'd smile at me."

"Might you fly a kite again now?"

"But I'm nearly fifty."

"Don't you have a son who would like to fly one?"

• • •

"Ricky, do you want to come and fly a kite with me on Saturday?"

Irene looked up. "Don't be stupid. How can he do that. Anyway, you wouldn't know what to do with a kite if it bit you."

Fred felt the stab, but he saw a look of such desperate hope in his son's eye that it made him bold. "I would Irene. Yes I would."

On Saturday morning Fred pushed his son's wheelchair up the hill at the park. They didn't speak, a lot was riding on this. There was a light breeze, no clouds. Ricky waited while Fred laid out the kite, going over how to launch it, letting out enough line. The kite would fly, the kite must fly. When Fred was ready to try, he held the kite up to the wind, with line slack in his hand, ready to let it out the instant the wind caught it. As he held it high, he was ten years old again waiting for the right breeze. Now. This one. Let go. And Fred let go. The kite was caught on the breeze, and moved easily into the air, twenty, thirty, a hundred feet of line paid out, and the kite sailed above them, a green diamond with three streamers as a tail.

"Alright Ricky?" said Fred, as he turned to his son. And Fred had such a smile on his face. He had never smiled like that in all his life. A grin that split the face in two. His lips were spread so wide in grinning it hurt his cheeks. He looked down at Ricky in the wheelchair. Ricky was smiling too, and there was a look of pride on Ricky's face. When he realised that his son was proud of him, Fred felt the stabbing pain in his chest. But now, it was a door opening inside his heart not a door locked shut. Fred held out the spindle at the end of the line to the boy in the wheelchair and said, "Here son, you fly it." As he did so, he felt as if a firework went off inside him.

• • •

"A peak experience," said Gillian Hoff when he told her about it. "Shall you go on, and fly more kites together?"

As he opened his mouth to say "yes," the floodgates opened and Fred cried the first tears of half a lifetime's pain. Watching Fred's weeping, listening to the scarcely bearable sound of a man sobbing from the deepest level of his being, Gillian knew that a new stage of healing had started. Each time a kite flew, the wounds of his life would at last be given light and air.

• • •

"What happened to you?" said Mr. Twaites at the hospital.

Fred thought of the time that Gillian talked about how

all his life Fred's feelings had tried to communicate with his mind, how his mind wouldn't listen, how Fred's body was the only one that would listen, and how drastic action had been needed to make him listen. He looked at Mr. Twaites and suddenly felt sorry for him. Instead of the dismissive and patronising authority he had seen before, now there was an overworked and bewildered man. It occurred to Fred they were about the same age; perhaps Mr. Twaites had a heart condition too.

"I've been flying kites," said Fred with a smile.

"Ah well, the fresh air has obviously done you good," said the consultant.

Fred smiled, and inside his heart was singing.

*Further Travels
with Henry*

Further Travels
with Henry

I FIRST PERFORMED my one man version of Shakespeare's *Henry V* at the Little Theatre on the Isle of Mull in the Hebrides. Then I toured the show from London to Sydney. I played in schools, community centres, churches, and studio theatres—any place where folk would sit still long enough.

I played all the parts—kings and bishops, princesses and paupers, and of course both the English and French armies. Gradually the clergy started to become more venerable and the soldiers less energetic, and I decided to put *Henry V* into my propbox for a last time and move on to other things. A few years ago, however, an opportunity arose for me to travel thousands of miles at my own expense to a place where I would not get paid, to revive the show and perform it for an audience of farmers. How could I resist?

This is how it all began. Sarah was an American theatre director visiting London. She and I met in London one winter, on a day exactly between our birthdays. I saw her in the foyer of the Central School of Speech and Drama.

"Who's that girl?" I asked my friend Michael.

"That's Sarah. I told you about her."

I turned to him to say, "That's the girl I'm going to marry." But I didn't say it for the very good reason that Michael's girlfriend Deborah was one of Sarah's best friends. Instead I asked him to introduce me. Three weeks later I popped the question. The day after the ceremony, Sarah had to go back to America to direct a play. For a while it had been marriage by phone.

"Come forward England if you want that phone," yelled the conductor. He was an ebullient man built on the American scale. We were on a train from New York City to Vermont, and the train got later and slower as the day went on. Each time I asked if we would arrive at three, or at four, or at five, the conductor's answer was the same, "Well it won't be any earlier." I made my phone call. I was on my way to join the Vermont Ensemble Theatre, with the basics of my show packed in two parcels wrapped in brown paper and tied with string. From my air conditioned comfort, I watched America go by, as the long double-decker silver train inclined towards the Hudson river, rounding the thickly wooded slopes of New York State. I enjoyed the exotic sounds of the place names as the conductor announced them, and it seemed to me that he spoke them with relish too, "Schenectady! Next Poughkeepsie. This is Lake Champlain!"

The stop in Vermont had no platform and no station. It was simply a sandy pause in the dense green. "Say!" said the conductor, as he passed down my parcels, "You're English right?"

"Yes."

"I knew you was English. English or Australian."

"Am I wearing a sign?" I thought.

"I was just there last year," he continued, "How about that Princess Di! She a good friend of yours?"

"Oh yes, we're very close."

"Funny, I didn't see you at the party."

He rang the bell and the train moved off toward Canada.

David, one of the theatre's coproducers was there to meet me. Taciturn, keen, firm handshake, clear eye. We got into his ancient Beetle (it was no surprise to learn it was called Herman) and took off. I looked around, and agreed that *New* England makes sense. Everywhere I looked was rougher version of the home counties. Woodland with spikier trees, herds of dairy cattle marked so brightly they seemed painted. And grain silos standing in fields like waiting rockets. David kept a brief commentary going as we lurched along. "This is Middlebury," he said. And indeed it was—a town of a few thousands with wooden clapboard houses all painted white and one main street leading to the town square with its three churches. "This is Main Street," said David, pointing out the soda fountain, the library, and the bar.

We hiccuped to a halt outside the company house. There was Sarah. Our life together as husband and wife could begin—or could it? It was to be a crowded summer. The house was big—large enough for maybe twelve people. The company was twenty-five people—plus a python and a macaw. This tiny menagerie were part of the cast of *La Strada*, an American debut that had required negotiations with Felini himself. The macaw was the loudest member of the company by far and yelled "Macaw!!!" over and over again from first light till well into the night.

The company house was convenient to all points in town. Across from the front door, there was a large green lawn giving on to trim streets of detached wooden houses. Within sight were the bicycle shop, the pool hall, the bakery, and the general store. And on all the horizons the swarthy hills bearded in green bristle. There was also a grocery store handy for the local ice cream, which is as good as the Italian variety. Not everyone was a stranger: Peter Risafi, whom I had known in his radical student days, was there too. He had been a year senior to me at the Central School of Speech and Drama, and our friendship had begun one day when he said to me "Can we get a coffee somewhere? I hate everyone in my year, and I've been through most of yours."

Eric Brandenburg, another Centralite, was also there—a bighearted man from Oregon with a voice like a cheese cutter. We had shared prawns in oyster sauce at midnight in London, and it was very good to see him again. The other coproducer—and founder of Vermont Ensemble Theatre—was Bess, a slender pixie who ran on fire and air. She zipped all over the state in her pickup truck conjuring sponsors out of the woods, arranging picnics for the company, and publicizing the theatre. She had been to school in London for a year, and we began to exchange greetings in each other's accents, her English one based on postwar British films. "Hello darling, will you have a sardine?"

In the mornings, the house would empty, and I would practice *Henry V*. Sometimes I took a bicycle and pedaled around the colleges, declaiming as I went. At the other end of Main Street, there were some huge neoclassical buildings built with the endowments of former students who had become Wall Street bankers. One morning as I was cycling around these buildings, a little boy about six years old waved me to a halt. I recognized him because he lived next door to the company house. "You speak Russian?" He said.

"No," I said.

"Yes." He was quite sure.

"I don't. Not at all."

"Sure you do," he said, as if he knew I was just kidding, and he spoke to me in Russian. After a few tries, when he saw that I really didn't understand, he told me to get off the bike; and we sat on the lawn as he taught me to count to ten. Adin, dva, tree, chteeri . . .

Lunch was supplied by the company. The food was plentiful, and starchy. Everybody drank some stange instant powdered brew called "tea" or "iced tea". I tried to explain. Really though, where do you start? Bess had arranged to use the local school as a refectory where we sat at long tables and there was loud chat. The company was composed of the technical crew who wore their hair long and their boots without laces, a group of teenage theatre enthusiasts who played small parts and assistant stage managed, and a band of New York–based actors who relished the chance to get out of the City and breathe clean air. At mealtimes, there always came a moment when Bess tapped a spoon on a glass and call out "Gripes!" Grievances could then be aired and shared. English reserve compelled me to remain silent on these occasions.

In the afternoons, I scurried around assembling the rest of my props. For Vermont I had prepared a half-hour version—with flags, streamers, confetti, and a red nose. As I put this together, I wondered nervously if I'd chosen the best play for this audience.

Some evenings my wife and I would cycle to the gorge where there were pools where we could swim—until the mosquitoes came. When they arrived, we went along the straight roads between the small communities past wheat fields, past corn fed cattle in the short, bright twilights. And everywhere we went, the grain silos stood in the fields. I tried to imagine them in Sussex and failed.

The theatre was based in Middlebury, but shows toured to the nearby towns. One summer, when the company offered *Our Town*, the whole of Middlebury had been the stage. This year *La Strada* took place in the fields behind the sports hall. For those shows needing a formal stage, a large marquee had been put up.

Sarah's first night was a play called *Blue Window*, a New York play, a sophisticated tale of urban loneliness. It went very well, and its success gave me heart for my own show, which I felt was even more incongruous in rural Vermont.

More people than I expected came to the first night of *Henry V*. The churchmen were played by three-quarter-size puppets suspended on coathangers from the propbox. A lit cigar became a cannon and supplied the smoke of war. A model ship on a strip of sea carried the English soldiers to France where Princess Katherine was a parasol in pink light. Heralds in paper airlines delivered messages, and at least one of the French soldiers sold onions from a bicycle.

"Into a thousand parts divide one man," says the text. Somehow, being two men at once was more difficult than being thousands. I found this out in staging one dispute between Henry and a soldier. I was obliged to put the custard pie in my own face

As a companion piece, I told the story of the Little Theatre on the Isle of Mull, and this provoked good resonance. Sitting in a marquee in a remote part of New England, it was easy to imagine a converted barn in a remote part of the Hebrides, and my audiences understood when I told them about the grazing midges there, because a brightly lit tent in Vermont in the summer attracts mosquitoes very effectively. Spray keeps most of them outside, but all through the show I heard the slaps of the bitten. Afterwards, a bunch of us (to use the vernacular) went to Mr. Ups, the local nightspot. While I was at the bar, a tall, bearded man came up to me and said, "Parlez-vous français?"

"Un peu."

He explained that he had seen the show and enjoyed it. I thanked him and asked, "Parlez-vous anglais?"

"Mais oui."

He went on to explain—in French—that he had just arrived that day for the language school. During the summer the colleges in Middlebury run short, intensive courses in

European languages, which they teach by total immersion. The students promise to speak nothing but their chosen language for the whole time, and in the streets and shops you hear snatches of the tongues of all nations. I took my bottle of Mexican beer and went out on to the deck to watch the river flow. The river runs perpendicular to Main Street and crosses it at about midtown. From there it falls fifty feet or so to the place where the bakery stands, a bakery famous for its sensational muffins. Outside the bakery a group of us would sometimes sit and swop audition stories.

"What's it like to be an actor in New York?" I asked my old friend Peter.

"It sucks," he said. "It sucks pond water."

And he told me about the audition where he was asked if he minded appearing in the nude. "I guess not," he said, "It would depend on the script." And how did he feel about tap dancing they had wanted to know.

"In the nude?" he asked.

Ellen McLoughlin, a playwright and actress, had once walked through a door to be greeted with the command, "Be a thumb."

I told them about the time in London, when even younger and keener than nowadays, I'd gatecrashed an audition. As I went through the doorway into the waiting room, I saw that the room was full of dwarves. Feeling that it would nevertheless be rude not to go in, I sat down in the only available chair. No one took any notice of me. Everyone else in the room was a dwarf. After a while, the door to the audition room opened and a man well over six feet tall came out. This was the director. He looked at me with a barely perceptible double take. "Yes?"

"Yes," I said, "I haven't got an appointment, but I wonder if you could see me."

"All right," he said "You may have to wait a while."

The audition continued, some of the dwarves were seen and went away, other dwarves arrived. Eventually, I turned to the small gentleman on my right. "What's the audition for?"

"*The Hobbit*," he said.

One evening I took *Henry V* to Blueberry Hill, high above Middlebury and deep in the forest. At dinner I sat opposite a lawyer from Mobile, Alabama. He was interested in me and I in him. Before long we were at it heart to heart in the American way, exchanging the details of our lives. He treated me—which I found at once charming and disconcerting—as though I were his best friend. After the show, we went outside to look at the sky. Against a backdrop of greens and scarlets we looked each other deep in the eyes, moved by intense and sudden friendship. We didn't speak, but the lawyer quietly put his hand on his heart. And in the stillness of the forest at sunset I understood why the actors from New York saved like misers for months to be able to come here and make fifty dollars a week. It was a long way from Broadway.

At the company house, the macaw was discovering new heights of volume. Sarah and I were offered the use of a house on the banks of a reservoir, surrounded by virgin forest. "You'd be all by yourselves," said our host.

"Great," we said.

The house stood at the end of an unpaved road, miles from anywhere. Miles from theatres, actors, and the public. It was balm to be alone in the silence. It was a great spot for a honeymoon.

We unpacked and took a swim in the reservoir. I had just put the kettle on to make tea—real tea—when the phone went. "Hi! Bob here." This was Bob's house. "An old college chum has some overspill from a wedding, and there may be one or two people stopping by. I can't believe it, this has never happened in twenty five years." That evening four adults and eight children arrived. They were friendly people, and another time it would have been fun to get to know them. We returned to Midllebury and the last night of *Blue Window*.

It was a great show. At the party afterwards, Peter Risafi asked me what I thought of my time in Middlebury. I told him I thought it was a "between place," where nationality could become blurred. I thought of my friend the little boy from Russia, of the language students who filled the streets with European sounds. I thought of the night when touring *Henry V* in the neighborhood, I'd driven ten miles on the wrong side of the road. I thought of waffles, butter pecan ice cream, blueberry muffins. As an Englishman amongst all this, and performing a classical text, I had developed a tendency to turn into Jeremy Irons. One day I took action and purchased a lumberjack shirt in an attempt to blend into the local landscape. Even so, walking along Main Street, feeling more English than ever, I was still convinced that I would never get the hang of New World ways. Then a visitor from out of state hailed me.

"Say, you look like you're from around here. Where's a good place to eat?"